ROYALS
AND ROGUES

Cynthia Smith

BERKLEY PRIME CRIME, NEW YORK

ROYALS AND ROGUES

A Berkley Prime Crime Book / published by arrangement with
the author

PRINTING HISTORY
Berkley Prime Crime edition / December 1998

The Penguin Putnam Inc. World Wide Web address is
http://www.penguinputnam.com

ISBN: 0-425-16643-0

Berkley Prime Crime Books are published
by The Berkley Publishing Group,
a member of Penguin Putnam Inc.,
375 Hudson Street, New York, New York 10014.
The name BERKLEY PRIME CRIME and the BERKLEY PRIME CRIME
design are trademarks belonging to Berkley Publishing Corporation.

PRINTED IN THE UNITED STATES OF AMERICA

10 9 8 7 6 5 4 3 2 1

For David, my favorite Russian, with love

My thanks to Ritva Muller and Marjariitta Giardina for helping me to really see and feel the unique qualities of their native Finland. I am most grateful to Detective Chief Superintendent Juha Keranen of Finland's National Board of Investigation for his invaluable instruction in the justice system of his country. Professor Igor Shturz was a charming and informative guide to his beloved Saint Petersburg. And most of all, special thanks to my very good friend Oleg Kapoustine who inspired the book and helped me with the accuracy of my facts and language throughout.

ROYALS
AND ROGUES

I

JUST AS I began to eat my beluga-caviar-covered baked potato, the usual first course at this year's elegant New York dinner parties, I felt a hand on my knee. When it began to move diagonally upward under the short skirt of my black satin Versace suit, I reached down, yanked up the traveling hand and slammed it into the plate of the elderly man at my right.

"Ellis," I said with a smile, "even you can't afford the toll to cross that bridge."

He roared with delight as he wiped eighty-five dollars' worth of caviar off his hand. Rebuff was not a common occurrence in the life of Ellis Brannock. Fifty billion dollars and the position of founder and sole owner of one of the world's largest communications empires did a far better job than cosmetic sur-

1

gery to make his wrinkles and wattles invisible to women of all ages.

We had met casually at other events on the New York elite circuit, which consisted of the biggest doers and donors in the city. The ticket of entry was big bucks given to the right charities, number one being the New York Public Library, formerly under the aegis of Brooke Astor, who was revered because she was the closest thing to old-money society in a town filled with money-come-latelies. Contributing a new wing to the Metropolitan Museum, bearing his-and-her-names of course, or donating your collection of nineteenth-century Impressionists to MOMA will also bring you acceptance. Since men who are brilliant financially tend to be dull socially, the group liven their activities by including achievers in the arts and beautiful people who pursue interesting professions. That's where I come in.

I find their endless glitzy balls and chic dinner parties to be terminally boring. But since the rich and famous are my source of income, I put on my designer gowns in the competition to display the most flesh admissible within the law, and mingle. The affairs are attended by the same people—women whose cosmetically tightened faces make them look like they're standing in the wake of a Concorde, and men whose thousand-dollar formal wear can't entirely camouflage the bulging guts and overflowing love handles.

Ellis Brannock was a bit of a maverick in the group because he chose to spend his billions for political and social causes rather than donate the money to create personal memorials. His Ellis Brannock Foundation was devoted to funding the economic revival of nations that had just emerged from the yoke of totalitarianism. Of all the guests at this dinner for thirty in a Fifth Avenue duplex penthouse, conveniently located two floors above my apartment, he was actually my preferred choice of dinner partners since his activities displayed a social conscience missing from the others in the room.

"Come on, Emma," he said after the meal was over, "let's go out on the terrace. I think we ought to get to know each other better."

There was no sexual innuendo in his invitation, which would have caused me to plead the urgent need to powder my nose. If there's anyone I find tedious, it's the raunchy old guy who assumes a beautiful exterior indicates an airhead interior which would assure acceptance of the advances of Godzilla if he had an eight-figure net worth. Ellis Brannock was a seventy-year-old slender short man. But as the joke goes, when he stands on his money, he's tall. His face had those deep vertical creases that add interest to a man's face and age to a woman's. There are those who might have found him attractive, especially with the confident aura of power that he exuded. I'm not one of them. Age doesn't enter into consideration in my friendships, but it does in my sexual relationships.

We sat down on the huge wraparound terrace and viewed the moonlit beauty of Central Park. Then he turned and eyed me carefully.

"I've heard about you," he said.

I smiled. "And I you."

He laughed. "Touché."

He looked at me with piercing shrewd eyes. "I am told you handle delicate matters with great discretion and competence. That you're very smart besides being extremely beautiful."

I nodded. "That pretty much covers it."

He grinned. "False modesty is a time-wasting stupidity. An intelligent person knows his or her own worth and just goes ahead and gets the job done."

"And what job is it that you want done, Ellis?"

"Am I being that obvious?" he asked.

"Maybe not to everyone, but I can always spot when a person has a problem he wants me to solve. I thought I might save us both the time of going through the polite thrust-and-parry ritual that will end up with you revealing all."

People tell me things. I apparently exude some sort of simpatico quality that makes them want to pour out their deepest feelings of disappointment, anger, fear, or anguish and turn to me for help. This man can command all sorts of resources to get him out of difficulty. But one drawback of such resources is they usually involve many people, which makes confidentiality difficult if not impossible. The need to coordinate multiple reports also increases the amount of time that will be spent on the project. I work alone, which guarantees secrecy, and I work fast. If I take on a case, I will spend no more than two weeks on it. Some people think I have some mystic reason for the number two. I have a reason, but it has nothing to do with phases of the moon or biorhythms. It's just that I am long on brains but very short on patience.

If a case interests me (I wouldn't take it unless it did) I'm ready to devote two weeks of my life to it. After that, it becomes boring and I'm out of there.

"I understand you claim never to have failed. Are you that brilliant?"

"Yes," I said with a smile. "But the real reason for my hundred percent success record is that I never take on a case unless I'm reasonably certain I can resolve it. Now, if that isn't proof of my intelligence, what is?"

He smiled and looked at me appraisingly. "You certainly don't look like a private eye."

"You've read some of those lady-shamus books and you expect me to have a wardrobe of jeans and sweats and exist on a marginal income in a tenement or a trailer—"

"And subsist on Big Macs and pizza," he finished with a hearty laugh.

I shook my head. "I'm sorry I don't fit your cliché concept . . . but actually I have an apartment in this building as well as a flat in London and a villa in Portugal. And the jeans in my closet hang next to my Diors and Givenchys. I'm not a P.I.—I'm a Private Resolver. It's a profession all my own."

"What's the difference?"

"A P.I. might be hired to find someone or something. I not only find the persons or objects, but resolve the situation that caused them to disappear."

"All in two weeks," he said.

"Or less," I added.

"At a fee of twenty thousand dollars, I heard," he said.

"Thirty thousand for you," I said.

"Why more for me? Just because I can afford it? I dislike fees that are based on the 'what the traffic will bear' formula."

"Ellis, all my clients can well afford my fee. To most of them, it's the equivalent of their monthly American Express card bills. I've upped yours because I sense your problem will entail extraordinary complications and dangers."

He sighed. "Well, as my teenage daughter would say, you got that right."

The girl must be the product of wife number two. The current number three was not much older than his daughter by wife number one and had just produced an infant son. I always wonder how these grizzled zillionaires whose nubile wives proudly present them with offspring are certain that it was their sperm that hit the jackpot. A woman can't fake maternity, but short of DNA, how can a man be sure of his fatherhood? Many an old geezer has publicly boasted a new birth to be proof of his heavy-duty testosterone when the occasion is privately regarded as proof of his cuckolding.

"It's my foundation, the one that distributes money to help emerging countries rebuild their business structures. Something's going on there that I sense is wrong. I need it checked into."

I was puzzled. "If funds are being mishandled, why not just send in your accountants to look over the books?"

He shook his head. "It's not that simple. The figures are fine. It's just that my sixth sense, the one that

6

never fails me, tells me that something sucks. Christ, I'm berating my daughter constantly to improve her language and here I am adopting it myself.''

I laughed. ''When I was in college, my mother was at me all the time about what she called my new vulgar vocabulary. She said she didn't consider *shit* and *fuck* to be acceptable generic adjectives and that slang is the recourse for lazy minds. But slang brings new life to old languages. Today's colloquialisms, if they're uniquely expressive, frequently enter the dictionary.''

''I have a solid board of trustees who run the foundation,'' he continued. ''All the members were hand-picked by me and are old friends or trusted business associates. I really have no specific accusation, just that something doesn't smell right. Right now our major funding is going to Russia.''

''Why there?'' I asked. ''Seems to me they're doing just peachy. The huge multinationals are all over the Russian landscape pouring money into that massive sinkhole. The oil companies seem to be vying to see who can deliver the most billions into the pockets of corrupt government officials and the Russian Mafia. I think they're all crazy. Why would you want to join in the big boondoggle?''

He shook his head. ''They're not crazy. Russia offers two tantalizing lures. First, they have an incredible supply of natural resources that have barely been tapped. Do you know that our submarines are armored with coats of titanium, but the Russian ones are solid titanium, they have so much of the stuff? And the oil—it's just sitting there waiting to be taken.

Cynthia Smith

The second attraction is the huge market of buyers. You realize how many potential cigarette smokers live there? The people are in trouble, struggling to learn how to make a living in a country that destroyed their work ethic by guaranteeing them wages just for showing up. When you're in trouble, you turn to the old supports of alcohol and nicotine. The largest signs in the St. Petersburg airport are of the Marlboro man. So the big corporations are willing to drop millions there to develop the resources and market. They're aware that many of their dollars are going to greedy corrupt officials and criminals. But that's merely regarded as part of the investment. Everyone wants to get a foothold early on and they're willing to give it time and whatever money it takes. It may seem like a terrific risk, but the payoff could be fantastic. Look at what McDonald's accomplished.''

''I've heard that the Big Mac is fast replacing borscht as the national food,'' I said.

''Don't scoff. You're not so far off. Not only did McDonald's change Russian eating habits, they revolutionized Russian farming. Russian potatoes didn't make the kind of french fries McDonald's wanted, so they distributed tubers of our kind of spuds to Russian farmers, who are now reaping big harvests and profits. Same with the cows; McDonald's showed them what kind of breeds they needed for American-style hamburgers, and voilà—everyone's making out.''

I was puzzled. ''But if oil and titanium are already being courted big time, and American businessmen with handfuls of dollars are more prevalent on the

Russian steppes than Volga boatmen, who needs you and what are you doing there?''

"Good question. We're there to help the little guy. Major industries are being handled, but I've always felt the backbone of a solid economy is small business. So we're sending in money and expertise to encourage that aspect of Russian development.''

"Anything specific?''

"The St. Petersburg Tsvetnuye Metalluy Company,'' he said with a lousy Russian accent. "It means 'colored metals' such as copper and aluminum. We're financing the development of a whole industry.''

"And your Russian baby isn't flourishing as expected?'' I asked.

He frowned. "Algie keeps giving me these glowing reports, but nothing is being produced and I have a gut feeling things just aren't kosher. He's the head of my board and an old friend . . . a very competent chap but not too great on communicating.''

"With a name that sounds like pond scum, I might not feel like talking too much either.''

He smiled. "Some parents don't consider a kid's future when they name him. His name is Algernon Dempsey.''

"What made the board pick this particular company to develop?''

"Algie is the retired CEO of Traverse Aluminum Ltd., so he'd naturally be attracted to an enterprise involving metals.''

"What do you want of me?'' I asked.

"I want you to infiltrate my board then go to Russia and find out what the hell's going on.''

"Infiltrate? Do I have a license to kill? Sounds like something out of John Le Carré or Ian Fleming.''

"I'm going to add you to the board. That's my right.''

"Come on, Ellis. They'll figure me for the company spy and clam up.''

I thought for a minute. "When I was a lawyer, I handled a Russian client for the firm.''

His eyes opened. "You're an attorney? What firm?''

I told him.

"Son of a bitch, that's my law firm. You'd have had to be pretty damned good to have made it with that bunch. What made you give it up?''

"I found out that slavery was outlawed in 1865. I used to watch the senior partners leave at three for their golf games at Winged Foot while I worked twelve hours a day, seven days a week to supply them with enough billable hours to support their lifestyles. I figured that went with the territory of building a successful law career. Sure, I made a lot of money, but I never had a minute to spend it. Then one day, while on a business trip to Denmark, I met an English Lady who told me about her involvement in a scandal that might rock the English aristocracy—as though they needed any help in that area. I told her I could fix it. For a fee.''

"She just poured out her innermost secrets to you, a stranger?'' he asked laconically.

"Didn't you?''

He threw back his head and laughed. "Emma

Rhodes, what a combination. Smart and sexy. I may consider making you wife number four.''

"I'm familiar with your record, Ellis. By the time you've used up wife number three, I'll be too old for your taste.''

"And did you solve the Lady's problem within two weeks?'' he asked.

"Actually, I'd figured it out within five minutes. But I told her I needed two weeks.''

"Why?''

"Everyone with a personal problem thinks it's the most serious, unique difficulty in the world. To have given her the answer within minutes would have trivialized the importance of her dilemma. Besides, if you get a job done too quickly, the client resents paying a sizable fee. You'll never get big bucks unless they think you've spent big time.''

"So you figured this was a hell of an easier way to make a living, and you chucked the law career?''

"Right.''

He nodded admiringly. "Smart move. Lawyers are a dime a dozen. But Private Resolvers are unique. What sort of legal matter did you handle involving Russians?''

"A merger between a Russian and American hockey team.''

"Negotiations must have been tough. I can't imagine a Russian hockey manager who could speak English.''

"He didn't. I learned Russian.''

He gaped. "To speak and read? The Cyrillic alphabet?''

11

I nodded. "In two weeks."

He smiled triumphantly. "One of my greatest talents is finding the right person for the right job. You're it for this one, Emma."

"I haven't said I'll take on the case yet, Ellis."

He smiled. "Of course you will. It's too great a challenge for you to turn down."

He was right.

"The next board meeting is Tuesday," he said.

"OK. I'll attend and leave for St. Petersburg Wednesday. I don't want to give them too much time to prepare my welcome."

II

IT WAS A small board, as those things go—only six members. Ellis had explained to me that he believed big boards produce little action since there are too many personal agendas that get in the way of productivity. They were seated around a round polished walnut table and all the men arose when I entered. Although their professional neon smiles tried to mask their resentment, they were obviously annoyed to have me join their little club.

Algernon Dempsey was hearty in his introduction and everyone greeted me politely, if not warmly. Hell, I would've been pissed off, too, if I were over sixty, as they all were, and the big boss arbitrarily dropped some ditsy-looking thirty-five-year-old on us who looked like she just stopped by between lunch and cocktails.

Cynthia Smith

I'm a great believer in clothes making the man or woman—that is, making you into anyone you choose to be at the moment. Appropriate dress for this occasion would have been a black suit, either Donna Karan or Chanel. That would have immediately placed me as one of them, only younger, and everyone would have immediately felt comfortable. Maybe almost slightly condescending and possibly even proprietary—you know, they'll soon teach their ways to this inexperienced respectful innocent. That was not the effect I sought. I wanted to create confusion, not comfort. Being regarded as a dumb broad makes people disregard you and speak freely. So I put on a Sonia Rykiel burnt orange, red, and blue printed wool sweater over a pink ribbed wool skirt that was slightly above mid-thigh. My brown hair was loose and shoulder length. I was wearing Shiseido's Petit Shadow Lemonade and Raspberry on Fire eye shadow and Clinique's Black Honey Almost Lipstick. My Manolo Blahnik shoes added two inches to my five feet, six inches. The instant reaction of the five men was a mixture of shock and leer. The one woman's face was easy to read—she hated me on sight.

Martina Albertson was the founder of the Martina Cosmetics empire, which produced some of the most expensive beauty products in the world. She was known in that cutthroat industry as well as on Wall Street for her creativity, shrewdness, and ruthlessness. Her navy-blue St. John's knit suit did a good job of hiding her obvious weight problem. Multiple face- and neck-lifts did a fair job of conveying a semblance

14

of youthfulness, but one look at those liver-spotted, wrinkled hands and the charade was over—the woman was obviously pushing seventy. How much easier it must have been when gloves were de rigueur, even indoors, for socially correct ladies.

"Well, how nice to have another woman on board," she said with a smile that was about as genuine as the huge zirconium ring on her finger. She was one of those wealthy women who maintain the myth of owning a priceless jewelry collection by flaunting excessive faux jewelry with the excuse that the real stuff is in the vault to protect her from predators. The dumb thing is that thieves don't go around with loupes in their eyes, and at a distance it's difficult to detect some of the skillful fakes from the real. I think I'd really be roiled to get mugged for a piece of paste. At least if they took the genuine article, I'd get satisfaction from the insurance company and make the front page of the New York *Post*.

"May I introduce you to your fellow board members?" she continued sweetly. She gestured toward the man next to her. "This is Red Wilkens."

He was a big burly Texan whose ol'-boy aw-shucks manner camouflaged a shrewd mind and a Harvard education. He was the retired CEO of an oil company he had founded, and had just made Texas headlines by contributing his tremendous collection of Frederic Remington sculpture to Southern Methodist University. I wondered where he got the name Red, since he had black hair, and I could see from the gleeful glint in his eye that he enjoyed the puzzlement his inappropriate name caused and was waiting for the inevitable question. I'd be damned if I'd give him the satisfaction. I later asked Ellis, who told me he picked up the sobriquet in his early days in the oil fields when he extinguished a huge fire and thus earned the nickname after the famous Red Adair.

"He loves to tell people the story. I must've heard it ten times, and he gets more heroic every time. He's made Red his official name because he hates his real one. Nobody knows it but me—and I'm sworn to secrecy, which I'll gladly violate if you ask me." I did, of course. "It's Igor. He was named after some remote Russian ancestor." That must've been hell to grow up with in Texas and I imagine school days do not conjure up dear-old-golden-rule days to him.

He shook my hand. "Delighted to meetya, Emma. Well, I sure think I'm gonna tell my pilot to fly lots faster when I come up for meetings now."

"And this is Richard Wrigley," continued Martina quickly, gesturing to the next in line. The CEO of a major insurance company, he was a small gray-looking man who was still gaping at me as he shook my hand. He stuttered a soft "How do you do?" and sank back into his chair. Ellis had told me to watch out for Wrigley. "He looks like an unimaginative bean counter with the kind of colorless face you forget while you're talking to him. That's what makes him so dangerous. Everyone underestimates him, but actually he's a ruthless son-of-a-bitch who would fire his own brother if it improved the bottom line. In fact, that's just what he did."

Tom Garrity was the shrewd Kennedy-style Irishman who had made his fortune in shipping after a

poor beginning on the docks. His sons now ran the
company he had founded, which was based in Boston.
His wife supported the local diocese and he supported
the topless bars in the Tenderloin. He owned a base-
ball team and wintered in Florida to be near their
training camp. He smiled at me as he shook my hand,
which he held far longer than necessary.

Bill Ephram was the intellectual New York millionaire banker who knew everyone in politics from
the White House down. His and his current wife's
social activities were constantly chronicled in *W* and
the *New York Times*. A short, portly man, his eyes
gleamed with intelligence and his face maintained an
amused expression, as though he were privy to some
joke that the rest of us were not.

After meeting them all, I was seated between the
last two men. A male secretary sat in the corner taking
notes.

"Dick, would you please get a pad and pen for Ms.
Rhodes?" asked Algie. I could hear from his tone that
he figured I'd probably use them strictly for doodling,
but the rules must be observed. From the hostile look
of Martina Albertson to the indulgently good-
humored look of the men, the group had sized me up
as Ellis's latest extramarital preoccupation, for whom
this incursion into big business was probably a titil-
lating reward for services rendered.

Live and learn, guys.

Algie called the meeting to order and they began
to discuss their Russian project. I listened quietly.

"Look, Algie," said Tom. "I know these things
take time, but for God's sakes, it's two years since

that plant was built, we keep pouring in big bucks, and we're still turning out nada. What the hell's going on there?''

Algie sighed. "I've told you before, Tom. Lomonosov is not Boston. You don't have a supply of skilled workers to draw upon. Plus the handicap that in Russia, getting labor to labor is difficult. They're just not used to it.''

"And what happened with that training group we sent over?'' Tom continued. "I never thought too much of those outfits who teach that motivation shit, if you'll pardon me, ladies.''

"It would never work in my business either," said Red. "Can you imagine pulling a bunch of guys off oil rigs to sit around and listen to some suit tell them how to develop a positive mind-set and have a nice day?''

"I thought it was an excellent idea," said Martina. "We've always found that psychological boosters help improve employee performance.''

A heated discussion broke out on the pros and cons of motivational training. Predictably, Red Wilkens and Tom Garrity mocked the entire concept. Richard Wrigley approved of it, and Bill Ephram took the intellectual's fair but action-deterring approach of seeing both the values and drawbacks of each side. Martina hotly supported Algie, as she apparently did on all issues. I wondered if there was more than a professional relationship between them. I had the suspicion there might have been once and she'd never gotten over it.

Apparently, a pile of dollars went into the motivation campaign, which, like other costly past attempts, had failed to improve the output of the Russian company. I listened to the heated battle going on about the lack of effectiveness of the recent effort, and tried to keep silent. But illogical analyses of a situation and ignorance of the obvious always infuriate me, and sometimes make me respond emotionally rather than rationally. And don't say that's typical of a woman. If Nixon had reacted logically instead of viscerally to Watergate, he might have ended his career in the glory instead of the gutter of public opinion.

"Did they speak Russian?" I asked.

There was a dead silence. They looked at me in shock. The airhead talks.

"Who?" asked Algernon.

"The people who were trying to teach the workers how to work," I answered.

"Well, no, of course not," said Algie. As though explaining to a child, he said, "They're Americans, employees of Ebsen, Inc., one of the largest labor-training communications companies in the country."

"Well then, how did they communicate?" I asked.

"There were interpreters, of course," said Algie impatiently.

"From Russia?" I asked.

"Of course. Did you expect them to come from Italy?" he asked sarcastically.

"I meant that Russian-speaking Americans might have been more effective in conveying strictly American ideas like motivation. From every session I've ever attended, the speaker's dedicated belief and enthusiasm were vital to whipping up audience acceptance. Since improving their productivity was never a concern under communism, all Russians needed to collect a paycheck was to show up, the concept is totally alien to them. There's no way a native Russian could summon up the kind of conviction needed to fire up Russian workers into changing their attitudes in order to increase output. No one ever gave a damn before and they'd need some pretty powerful persuasion to care now.''

They all stared at me in stupefied silence, except for Bill Ephram, who had a little smile on his face.

Well, there goes my whole image—I was now a brain in bimbo's clothing. I know, I shouldn't have allowed myself the luxury of voicing an intelligent opinion, but if I ever intended to cause confusion in the ranks, I sure as hell did that. The fun and challenge of my work is its unpredictability. So let's see how this little surprise plays out.

It was Bill Ephram who spoke first. ''What exactly is your professional background, Emma?''

''Law,'' and I named the firm. ''I handled M&A— mergers and acquisitions—and industrial start-ups.''

There were gasps and Martina looked ill.

''I suggest,'' said Bill ''that we send Emma to Lomonosov to get a complete lay of the land.'' He looked at me. ''I think she's got the three things to be the perfect person for the job—looks, brains, and youth.''

Bingo! Here I thought I'd have to go through all sorts of machinations in order to have the board send me to Russia, and now that's what's happening, and it wasn't even my idea. That's why I never spend time on elaborate planning. So often things just seem to come about by themselves. Of course, I made all the necessary protestations of my limited time and enthusiasm for the project, followed by the ultimate yielding to the needs of the board and the good of the Foundation. Oh, I was an absolute saint.

"I second the motion," said Tom. "I think it's time one of us went over there and it sure as hell ain't gonna be me. That one visit when we first opened the operation was enough for me. Hell, I like cabbage with my corned beef, but they serve it with everything except ice cream."

"The place is dangerous," said Richard. "The way the Russian Mafia guns down men, women, and children, they make the Godfather look like Pope Paul. That's just a bit too much to handle for folks our age."

I thought Martina would turn purple. I bet she wouldn't join AARP for fear the mailman would know she was definitely over fifty. I stole a glance at Algernon. There were so many emotions flitting over his face that I gave up after Apprehension and Confusion.

They took a vote about sending me to Russia—it was six to one in favor (guess who was the *nyet* vote? Martina, of course). If you haven't gathered, she's not from the "sisterhood" school of female interrelations. In her day, women never supported but rather regarded each other as competitors.

I was quite pleased with the way things had progressed. It's another example of the Emma Rhodes modus operandi, which is to enter a case with just a vague theory as to how to proceed. A carved-in-stone plan limits you and impedes freedom of choice. You could call it the "roll with it" or "seat of the pants" technique, but all it means is to hang loose so that you can take advantage of a situation as it develops.

"Good luck," said Tom Garrity as we were leaving. "That Ellis is quite a fella," he added with a leer and a chuckle.

When I phoned Ellis to tell him the results of the meeting, he said, "I heard all about it. You did one helluva job, my girl. They think it was their idea to send you to Russia, which solves the problem of trying to explain my doing it, and it also preserves my promised 'hands off' treatment of the board."

"I think I also did a bit for your 'hands on' image," I said.

He laughed. "Right. Now they think I'm making it with a classy gal who's got big brains instead of big boobs. Not that I wish to in any way imply that your body is less than gorgeous, Emma."

"Thanks, Ellis. I'll use you as reference when I enter the Ms. America contest in the thirty-and-over category. Right now I need a visa to Russia, which I understand takes at least a week and which I'm sure you can get overnight. The Russian embassy also requires a confirmed hotel reservation. Do they think I'm going there planning to sleep in the streets? But that's probably a carryover from the totalitarian government, which had to know where every foreigner was at all times."

"Not to worry, Emma, I'll take care of everything. My pilot will hand you all the necessary papers tomorrow when you board my plane. I know you don't require expense money when you're on a case, but let this one be an exception. I don't want you to be slowed down by the hesitation that affects people who are using their own money."

"You got the wrong girl, Ellis. To spend or not to spend is never part of my soliloquies. But I don't need your money, thank you."

"There will be a packet of dollars in varied denominations in the pilot's package. Rubles are useless. Everyone prefers dollars. If you need any more, just phone me." He plowed on with his little speech as if I hadn't spoken. "I also don't want to hold you to your usual two-week limitation. I'd like you to stay there as long as you think the situation requires—at my expense, of course. I'm not concerned with your making a point professionally."

It was a nice vote of confidence, but I don't keep to the two-week time frame to make points. I do it because I've never encountered any problem, no matter how critical it may seem to the client, that I haven't been able to settle within that time. Or even more important, one that could sustain my interest for any longer. I've told you I have very little patience. I also have a very big zest for living and I'm loath to allow work to cut into that. Two weeks, folks, and I'm out of there.

I won't bother arguing with him about taking his money; there's no point to it. I'll just leave it with the pilot. Men like Ellis Brannock cannot accept a no and just tune out other people's opinions. Money incurs obligation, something I won't allow. What I like best about my work is that I am totally independent and take orders from no one. Once you take a nickel from a client, you're in his pocket. You owe him.

III

FLYING TO EUROPE in a private jet has got to be one of the highest forms of sybaritic living and I reveled in it. No waiting around the airport for hours; the plane is waiting for you. No sitting at the gate listening for the attendants to call out your row for boarding. No standing in the aisle while some inept jerk holds up the line as he tries to shove his steamer trunk into the overhead bin. No trying to eat your food when the charmer in front of you has pushed his seat into the fully reclining position. No need to agonize over the choice between an aisle or window seat. Even flying first or business class has its drawbacks. You usually have a cabin filled with middle-management businessmen who wallow in the luxury of a change from tuna casserole and beer to duck breast and champagne with cognac chasers, and this results in a small area filled with sloppy drunks with dyspepsia. In other words, a private jet gives you the benefit of speed, which to me is the sole advantage of flying, with none of the irritations. And glory be, the food actually tastes like food and not Play-Doh. If you think I'm making too much of the importance of this up-in-the-sky luxury, let me rate it for you on the Emma Rhodes Scale of Pleasures and see how it compares with yours. In my book, it's right up there with lolling naked in a cool Jacuzzi under a hot sunny clear sky in Sedona. And biting into a two-inch-high hot pastrami sandwich on fresh seeded rye in the Second Avenue Deli in New York City.

The plane ride was pleasant and thus seemingly short. We put down at Pulkovo Airport in St. Petersburg. I took a cab into town, but not to the Grand Hotel Europe, where Ellis had booked me a room. It's a five-star luxury establishment, but it had two things against it—it was a hotel and Ellis would know I was there. I know men like Ellis—if you work for them, they feel they own you. They feel perfectly free to phone you at any hour, day or night, with whatever trivial question they want answered right then. I suspect they do it deliberately as a show of power. If you're being wheeled in for a quadruple bypass, you damned well better keep your cellular phone on the gurney in case *he* wants to ask you how yesterday's meeting went. To their employees, they are gods. Their method of enslaving people is predatory, and simplicity itself—they pay extraordinarily well in order to hook the recipients on a high standard of living. The fear of losing their luxurious perks turns them into toadies who will take any abuse their employer inflicts.

The thing I love about being a Private Resolver is that I work for no one but me. Since I demand no advance or per diem, I owe my clients squat. Most of these tycoon types are insomniacs who are consumed twenty-four hours with working out ways to make another billion or two. I do not want to be bugged by Ellis whenever he gets the whim to chat or check up on me. I would not be staying at the Grand Hotel Europe. I had made other plans.

As the cab drove into the city I looked around carefully, since I had never before been in St. Petersburg. After the city's years under a totalitarian regime that had little concern for anything other than functionalism, and now a government that claimed to have little money for anything more than survival, I was expecting to see decrepit buildings and South Bronx desolation. To my delighted surprise, our route took us along wide tree-lined boulevards flanked by graceful old buildings that were obviously low-rise apartment houses. Externally, they presented a look of beautifully maintained antique architecture. I was puzzled. If the country was in such a state of economic disaster, who could afford to live in all these elegant buildings? I found out later—and that's when you'll find out.

Along the way, there were the huge memorial statues of men in poses of heroes leading the masses. The parks in which they stood, however, were shabby and unkempt, with weeds and uncut grass. On many corners, I noted babushka-covered women with makeshift stalls selling rather meager piles of fruits and vegetables. The people on the streets were poorly dressed, most carrying shopping bags, and seemed to trudge rather than walk.

But nothing could detract from the beauty of the water. St. Petersburg is crisscrossed by more than sixty rivers and canals, giving it the name of the Venice of the North. The buildings that line the river are of softly colored stone that give an enchanted watercolor look in the early-morning sun.

My cab drove along the embankment of the Neva River, an important body of water that reaches the Gulf of Finland. Suddenly we came upon a huge magnificent pale green, gold, and white building that stretched for blocks along the quay. The Hermitage— the internationally famous museum that houses one of the most incredible collections of old and new masters and artifacts representing a myriad of cultures. Architecturally, it was classic Russian Baroque, which requires abundant sculpture and decoration and an invariable two-colored paint pattern. I looked at the surrounding skyline, which seemed to be totally horizontal, except for a few church spires. Then I remembered that Czar Nicholas II had decreed that no building could be higher than the Winter Palace, now the Hermitage. The building was begun in 1754 by Peter the Great's daughter Elizabeth, who wanted it to demonstrate the power of Russia, and was completed during the reign of the infamous Catherine the Great. Artists know how to project power with design, the rich know only to do it with size. The palace has 1,057 rooms and covers an area of 500,000 square feet. It is truly overwhelming, as it was meant to be.

Just a few blocks past it, the cab stopped in front of an elegant yellow stone three-story mansion.

"Is this it?" I asked.

"Number twelve Kutuzov's Nabereshnaya," the driver said as he got out to open the trunk to unload my luggage. *Nabereshnaya* is "riverbank." The front door opened and two men came out.

"Emmitchka." Prince Oleg kissed me and ordered his servant to bring my bags inside. He turned to the cabdriver. *"Skolka?"* How much?

The driver looked at the tall handsome gray-bearded man who was obviously someone of consequence and mentioned a figure that was half what he quoted to me at the airport. The prince snorted indignantly and mentioned a figure that was half that. The driver nodded reluctantly. I stepped forward to pay and the prince waved me away.

"Nichivoh." It's nothing.

I entered the front door and stopped. "Oleg—this is marvelous!"

We were in a grand hall with a domed ceiling filled with gold-encircled scenes of cherubs and angels. The room had niches containing bronze statues of saints and urns. In the center of the hall was a huge round table with an intricately carved gilt-encrusted base; a huge black sculptured vase filled with brilliantly colored flowers stood atop it. To the left was a wide gracefully curved staircase bearing the descending figure of a slim white-haired woman.

"Emmitchka—darling. How wonderful to see you. Welcome to our home."

It was Oleg's wife, the Princess Katrina. She had

the kind of fragile beauty that makes you a knockout when you're young and elegant when you're old. She was wearing a black-and-red-trimmed Chanel suit from the days when Coco herself did the designing.

We kissed the air around each other's cheeks in European style and I said, "And some home it is, Katrina. This place is magnificent."

Oleg told the servant to bring my bags upstairs and he walked over and put his arm around his wife, looking at her fondly. "Yes, we were most fortunate to be able to buy it. When my family was forced to leave Russia, we thought we would never come back. But when the communists left, we thought, 'Why not?' "

"But, Oleg," I said. "You seemed so settled and content in Estoril."

They had been part of the large group of exiled royalty who lived in Portugal. The Romanovs, Prince Michael of Greece, and many others lived in luxurious comfort in Estoril, an elegant suburb of Lisbon. Oleg and Katrina visited me often in the Algarve and frequently stayed in my Fifth Avenue apartment when they came to New York.

"We were happy there. But we have Russian souls and Russian hearts. In Portugal, we were visitors, no matter how many years we lived there. This is our homeland. Here we feel we belong."

"Come, you must have tea," said Katrina. "Marushka will unpack for you and then you can go upstairs and rest."

She led us into the salon, another glorious room with tall windows facing the river. I gasped with delight when a huge liner sailed slowly by.

"Ah, you like our moving murals," said the prince.

"The Neva gives us an ever-changing scene. I some-times sit in here for hours. It is a room that never allows one to become bored."

Another servant came in and set down a huge silver tray in front of the green silken damask sofa on which Katrina was seated. She patted the place next to her, inviting me to sit there as she began to pour tea. There was no question about milk or lemon; this was Russia, tea here is served with lemon. Along with the delicate cups on the tray was a tall glass of what looked like iced tea. Katrina smiled apologetically.

"I'm afraid Raya thinks all Americans like their tea cold. Of course, you may have it if you wish."

I declined the offer and she filled a cup and then put a small pastry on my plate.

"Now I know you young women turn away from desserts, but you must have one of Raya's famous *vatrushki*." She smiled at the woman who had brought the tea. "What can hurt you? It's made of cottage cheese, that food dieters eat."

I bit into one; it was delicious. "Mmm—plus a couple of other ingredients like sour cream, sugar, raisins, vanilla, and eggs. Right?" I looked at Raya and said in Russian, "These are marvelous. How do you make them?"

Her heavily wrinkled face broke out into a broad smile displaying two gold teeth. As I figured, it was the kind of simple recipe that meets the Emma Rhodes prerequisite: the list of ingredients must be no longer than one inch, the instructions no more than one and a half inches. I like to cook, but not if it seriously cuts into my life. I have friends whose idea of pleasure is to spend two days shopping for and one day cooking a meal that gets consumed within thirty minutes. The ratio makes no sense to me.

In case you want to try it, here goes: one pound cottage cheese, two eggs, four tablespoons sugar, one tablespoon sour cream, one quarter cup of raisins, a half teaspoon vanilla, pinch of salt. Drain the cheese and rub through a sieve. Mix with other ingredients. Roll out a pie crust thin and cut it into three-inch rounds. Place mixture in center of each round, pinch edges to make border, keeping top open. Bake in 350-degree oven until pastry browns.

As I sipped my tea I asked more about the house. "I thought the government didn't allow private homes—one building lived in by a single owner."

"Yeltsin's privatization has changed much," said Prince Oleg. "But the big breakthrough came last year when Rostropovich bought a house here on the Kutuzov's Nabereshnaya, all for him and his family. A sensation was caused, not only because he chose to leave Moscow for St. Petersburg, but because the house is not a communal residence but is solely for his family. It is just down the river from here. So I said to my Katrinitchka—why not us? This city had been my family's home for generations. Our palace in Pushkin was destroyed years ago, either by the communists or the Germans. Then this house became available—the government had been using it as a library for communist works and the caretaker and his family lived on the second floor. The place was a disaster. It was once the home of one of the czar's cousins and the so-called people's government saw no reason to maintain what they considered examples of royal excesses, so they allowed it to deteriorate dreadfully. In their blind fanaticism, they overlooked the fact that this and other buildings like it are part of our national heritage—examples of Russian artistry. I had some money and our son, Prince Aleksei, is a very astute businessman with many interests here and was able to add the rest. He was very clever about working through the endless bureaucracy so that we were able to make the purchase. Of course, he spent a sizable amount to restore it, but I believe it's worth it, don't you?"

"Yes indeed," I said.

The door to the room opened and a tall, thirtyish, brown-haired man with a mustache and Vandyke beard in the style of Czar Nicholas came in. Aha, the young prince. He was strikingly handsome and was dressed in strictly Savile Row. This trip may present other areas of interest besides business.

"Aleksei!" said Katrina with a big smile. "Come in and meet our houseguest."

Hot damn if he didn't kiss my hand and hold it. He was too young for this sort of period gallantry, so either he was pulling my leg or he'd been watching too many old movies. When he looked up at me, the twinkle indicated he was obviously playing out the role of courtly nobility. I dropped to the floor in a deep curtsy, looked down demurely, and said, "Your highness."

His parents roared and his father said, "Aleksei, I do believe you have met your match. This is Emma Rhodes."

"Enchanted—and I mean it," he said. The look in his eye indicated he was already assessing the possible proximity of our rooms.

"Come and join us for tea," said his mother, and he pulled up what looked like an authentic Biedermeier chair facing me.

"What good fortune for us brings you to St. Petersburg, Emma?" he asked as he bit into a pastry.

"I think that may be an indiscreet question, Aleksei," said Princess Katrina. "Emma handles private affairs for people, very effectively I've been told by some of our friends. I don't think we should ask her about her business."

Aleksei looked at me appraisingly with a slightly mocking smile. "You mean like finding missing jewelry and husbands?"

Sometimes my appearance works advantageously for me. I was wearing my newest Claude Montana tan pantsuit. It's soft, pleasant, comfortable for traveling and obviously couturier-created to someone who knew fashion, as Aleksei apparently did. He figured a beautiful high-style woman (it's not conceit, just factual) is someone not to be taken too seriously. I'm always ambivalent about that sort of reaction. On the one hand, I was pleased my little charade worked to deflect interest in my profession; on the other hand, I felt like kicking him in the balls.

"How about your business, Aleksei? I gather you have interests here in St. Petersburg. Wouldn't that have been somewhat difficult for 'white Russians'—descendants of the oppressive czars and enemies of the state?"

"Communism is no longer the form of government here," he said.

"Yes, but communist attitudes don't change that fast. The people must still care."

"All the people care about today is having enough to eat," he said wryly. "Fighting the class struggle is a luxury you can't afford when you can't feed your family."

"Aleksei has a degree from your Wharton School," said Oleg. "He has always been involved in high-level business activities—and quite successful at it," he said proudly.

"What could be more natural than bringing his expertise and talents to his homeland?" said his mother.

Aleksei smiled. "Thank you for your vote of confidence," he said, looking at his parents fondly.

Being involved in high-level business activities here in Russia requires expertise they don't teach at Wharton—yet. I don't believe the curriculum offers "Bribery I and II" or "Corruption: An Invaluable Business Tool." Maybe I was judging him unfairly and he operated within the rules. Maybe. Anyway, I could see that he loved his parents, and if you've read any of my books, you know I like that in a man.

I stifled a yawn and said apologetically, "Sorry, jet lag. I truly understand how torturers use sleep deprivation as a weapon. Right now I think I'd admit to murdering Rasputin if I could get to bed."

Katrina jumped up. "Oh my dear, of course. I'm so sorry. You are so lively and engaging, it's hard to realize that you must be aching to rest. Come, let me show you to your room."

We walked up the majestic staircase to the second floor and she led me down a deep-burgundy carpeted hall lined with ancestral portraits. Their severity was softened by the few small tables along the way bearing vases of flowers. She threw open a door and led me into a charming room that I couldn't admire properly through my closing eyes. She saw me look longingly at my nightgown, resting upon the pillow. I always wear one in other people's houses—not only to observe the decencies, but because I don't know the quality of their sheets. I may sound like the princess and the pea, but I'm used to Porthault sheets, which cost the earth—a thousand dollars per sheet last time I bought some—but are incredibly delicious to have next to your bare skin.

Katrina looked at me sympathetically. "Cocktails at six, and we do not dress for dinner, my dear," she said. And she walked out, closing the door behind her.

I awoke three hours later and hopped under a shower. There was an array of toiletries on the marble table next to the sink. I looked at the labels; they were Martina Cosmetics. I was glad my hosts' new love affair with the motherland didn't extend to its products. I had heard that Russian shampoo created neither lather nor cleanliness and the toilet paper was excellent for shining shoes.

I came downstairs and walked into the salon exactly at six. When the princess told me they didn't dress for dinner, that didn't mean jeans were acceptable. I wore a Givenchy pink silk two-piece dress with balloon push-up sleeves and a long slit up the skirt front. "Don't dress" means deep-six the diamonds and tiaras. But you can't go wrong with pearls;

I wore one strand of white and one of black. I felt refreshed and starved.

"Emma, you look lovely," said Prince Oleg as he came forth to greet me. "Please, would you like some champagne and caviar?" He motioned to Marushka, who was carrying a tray. "And then I want you to meet someone."

As I sipped my champagne he brought over a beautiful young woman. Straight brown hair cascaded down the back of her simple black sheath. Huge brown eyes stood out against her pale face; she looked to be in her late twenties, still at an age to get away with no makeup other than lipstick.

"Emma, this is my niece the Countess Irina."

"It's lovely to meet you," she said with a shining smile. I liked her immediately. "I've heard so much about you, I've been dying to meet you." Now I really liked her. "Let's sit down and talk." She led me to a couch.

Just as we got settled Aleksei came in and, after a quick survey of the room, walked over to us and pulled up a chair.

"Surely I've got to be sitting with the two most beautiful women in St. Petersburg. How lucky can I get?" He beckoned to Marushka, who was carrying a tray of blini, those marvelous little buckwheat pancakes with salmon-roe caviar. "May I make a plate for you, Emma?"

He put two on the plate and then, noting my apparently unsuccessful attempt to suppress my voracious anticipation, he added two more, each with the appropriate dollop of *smetana* (sour cream).

"I think you and I had better chat a bit, cousin, while our ravenous friend demolishes her blini. We mustn't forget she's flown the ocean today, and according to her internal clock, it's probably breakfast time."

I looked at him gratefully. With a mouthful of sour cream, it was hard to do anything but nod.

"Aleksei, I adore you, but I wanted to speak to Emma alone," said Irina with a pretend pout.

"What could you be speaking about to her that I couldn't hear?" he asked. "When we played together as children, we always told each other everything."

"Darling cousin," she replied, "as I remember, the last confidence I shared with you was when I got my period. You would be surprised at the many things I haven't confided in you since then." Then she looked at him intently. "And I suspect you, too, have many secrets from me."

What was going on here? Unsaid things are usually far more interesting than the spoken words. There were currents between these two that were intriguing and might or not be meaningful. For the moment I decided to toss the fact into my mental hopper to be retrieved at the appropriate moment. That's the way I work. Actually, so does Miss Marple. Solving problems involves compiling data that is held in your head until the facts start to connect.

Aleksei arose and bowed to Irina graciously. "O.K., cousin. I shall honor your wishes. But I shall be back. I, too, have things to discuss with Emma"— he looked at me—"in private." He walked over to greet his father.

"I really didn't intend to sound mysterious, but I wanted to ask about your work," Irina began.

Uh-oh. I hope I'm not going to be treated to an outpouring of personal problems. I couldn't handle another case right now, and if she was looking for free advice, I didn't do pro bono. People who ask doctors and lawyers at dinner parties for diagnoses and recommendations should know that advice given for nothing is worth just that.

"Actually, it's about Aleksei. I'm worried about him."

"Emma and Irina, may I introduce you both to someone?"

It was Princess Katrina, who was standing with a blond, trim athletic young man whom I recognized immediately.

I jumped to my feet. "But surely he needs no introduction," I said. I held out my hand. "I'm truly honored to meet you."

It was Dmitri Thomasov, the Olympic Gold figure-skating champion.

"I saw you perform in Lillehammer. You were incredible," I said. Irina had risen to her feet as well. The Russians take their ice skating seriously, especially these days, when the country is so severely lacking in heroes. Their computer scientists have gone to Stanford University, their pianists and violinists have gone to Carnegie Hall, and their ballet dancers are now in companies all over the United States.

I was eager to hear about Dmitri's life, and to escape from what I anticipated would be an awkward discussion with Irina. "Are you here to train for the next Winter Games?" I asked.

He grimaced. "Yes, but it is most difficult," he replied.

"How so?" I asked.

We sat down and he reached for a portion of caviar being offered by Marushka. I noticed the Russians serve it in its pure form, as I do—plain on buttered white bread. I have never understood why anyone would want to bury the delicate taste of those luscious black eggs with the strong flavors of onions, chopped egg, or brown bread.

"It is difficult, so difficult." He sighed. "We do not have anywhere to practice. We have our ice rinks as before, yes, but they are not as before."

"What do you mean?" I asked.

He made a sour face. "Last month, the electricity failed, so we had to end up skating in the dark. This happens frequently, because the bill has not been paid. There is very often no gas to run the Zamboni machine that resurfaces the ice. Many times I have had to pay for it myself. Sometimes we just have to skate on rutted, unprepared ice because the Zamboni driver won't work because he has not been paid."

"But ice skating is one of the prides of Russia. Your skaters won every figure-skating event in Lillehammer. How could they let this happen?" I asked.

He rubbed his two fingers together in the international gesture for money. "A rink in Nevinmomyssk has become a parking garage. The rink in Odessa where Victor Petrenko used to train is being demolished because the land has become more valuable to developers than the building.''

''That's a shame. At that rate, you'll soon lose your world dominance.''

Irina, who had been listening quietly, said sharply. ''We have become a country where greed overcomes pride.''

Dmitri nodded. ''Many of our coaches and skaters have gone to the United States. A top-level coach here maybe makes two hundred to three hundred dollars a month. In the U.S., they make one hundred to a hundred and fifty dollars an hour. Marina Eltsova, who won the 1996 world pairs championship with her partner, Andrei Bushkov, is planning to leave for America, for, as she puts it, better ice and a better life.''

''Is your coach still here?'' I asked.

''He was killed last month.''

I heard Irina gasp.

''Another coach was killed last week. The head of our hockey federation was recently murdered.''

Good Lord—that's the man I worked with to arrange the merger. ''Who and why?'' I asked.

He threw up his hands. ''Who else? The Mafia.''

He was not referring to the Sicilian or American organizations. Russia now has the distinction of having its own.

''The coaches were involved in some business deals that involved the Mafia, as almost all business here does. We are all a little scared and nervous. We try to tell ourselves that we are in sports not business and these hoodlums will not bother us. But that is no longer true. Hockey is big business. All sports are.

Our Olympic swimming champion, Aleksandr Popov, was stabbed recently.''

''Are you thinking of going to the United States?'' I asked.

''I would like to stay. We have a great skating tradition here. I love Russia. I love the country, I love the language, I love the people. My family is here, my friends are here. I have a nice home and I would like to bring up my children here, with their grandparents and uncles, aunts, and cousins around them. But if it comes to the point where I can no longer give them the life I wish, we will leave. Maybe we would be able to come back someday when everything straightens out.''

''Where do you train now?'' I asked.

''A small town near here called Lomonosov.''

I didn't blink an eye but I couldn't believe my luck. Lomonosov—my destination.

''They have a rink that was built many years ago for the workers in the big factory there. Some big Americans have taken over the plant now. Fortunately, they seem to respect our skating and take very good care of the ice.''

I'm sure Ellis would be delighted to know that he was paying to support the Russian skating tradition. ''Could I come and watch you practice?'' I asked with the smile that never fails.

He looked pleased and flattered. ''But of course. I am going there tomorrow for the day. But how will you occupy yourself—you would not enjoy watching skating for many hours.''

''No problem,'' I said. ''I've been dying to visit

the famous science museum of Lomonosov. I understand they have exhibitions of Russian astronomy and scientific devices and other work by the famous eighteenth-century scientist Mikhail Lomonosov, for whom the town was named.''

Dmitri looked suitably impressed and I thanked whatever gene gave me a photographic memory. I had boned up on the plane with a St. Petersburg guidebook I picked up at the airport. Somewhere among the listings of over twenty ''things to see'' that I usually avoid like the plague when traveling was a small write-up on the Museum of Lomonosov. I recall it nestled between two other hot ''don't miss'' winners, the Museum of Ethnography and the Military Historical Museum of Artillery, Engineering, and Communication Forces.

He smiled broadly. ''Ah, you are interested in science.''

Actually, it's the one section of the *New York Times* that I skip consistently. Anything to do with mathematics and science and my mind goes into automatic shutdown.

''Oh, very much,'' I said with an answering display of teeth.

We arranged that he would pick me up at eight-thirty the following morning.

Aleksei came over to lead us in to dinner. We entered the dining room, which was in the rear part of the house, facing formal gardens. But one hardly noticed the lovely view because of the striking impact of the interior. It was classic Russian Baroque. The walls were bright turquoise silk with row after row of gold-edged white columns. Between the columns were Della Robbia glazed terra-cotta reliefs of the annunciation of the Virgin, alternating with carved gilt mirrors. Six glittering crystal chandeliers suspended from the carved ceiling gave the room a sparkling festive look. The long fruitwood table was surrounded with Louis XIV gilt chairs carved with acanthus leaves and flower heads. I fully expected to see Czar Nicholas at the head of the table, but it was Prince Oleg beckoning for each of us to be seated. An aristocratic couple I had not seen before stood flanking him at the table.

"Emma, I don't believe you have met my brother and dear sister-in-law, Prince Mikhail and Princess Tatyana." We smiled and said the proper things to each other and then sat down. I hoped the dinner would be the cuisine of the country.

As though reading my mind, Princess Katrina announced to the table, "You may all thank Emma for the fact that tonight we must all forget our concern about fat and cholesterol. In honor of our American friend, I asked Raya to cook us a faithfully Russian dinner. When visitors come to our country, they want to dine on our food. If they wish French food, they go to Paris. So I give all of you permission to be totally guilt-free tonight. We have a good excuse." She smiled at me.

The first course was *shchi,* the classic hearty cabbage-and-vegetable soup served with heavy grain bread. This was followed by *bitki,* little codfish cakes with a mustard sauce. The entrée was Caucasian *shashlik,* which was marvelous. When I later asked

Raya how she prepared it, she told me the secret was to marinate the cubes of lamb for four hours in a mixture of lemon juice (one lemon per pound of meat), a quarter cup of red wine, two cloves of pureed garlic, one bunch of parsley and one bunch of dill, both chopped fine, salt, and pepper. The meat is then skewered, grilled, and served on a bed of rice. Mushrooms in sour cream and broiled eggplant completed the course. The dessert was *sabionov,* which is the Russian version of zabaglione, a delicate mix of egg yolks, sugar, lemon juice and rind, white wine, and rum, cooked together over a double boiler. Wonderful wine accompanied every course. I was glad the princess had not carried her only-Russian policy to the wine. We were drinking Château Margaux. The one time I tasted Russian wine, I recognized the origin of Manischewitz Concord Grape.

Everyone groaned with delight as each course reached the table. At the end of the meal, Aleksei rose and raised his glass. "To you, Emma, for creating the occasion that took us all back to our roots. I have not had a marvelous meal like this since my babushka cooked it for us when we were in the nursery."

Everyone laughed, especially his mother, who said, "Nonsense, Aleksei, you never had a babushka. We always had an English nanny for you."

"Please, Mama, you are ruining my story," he said in mock exasperation.

We all struggled up from the table and went into the salon to await the arrival of tea. With today's emphasis on lean cuisine, no one was accustomed to such a large meal and we were all sprawled out in various degrees of stupor.

"How did they do this every night?" Irina asked the room at large. No one had to be told what she meant.

"That's easy," I said. "They didn't have *Vogue* and *Harper's Bazaar* filled with pages of anorexic women. If you look at the paintings of nineteenth-century beauties, they'd be classified today as Stylish Stouts."

"If you think this is a lot of food, wait until the Easter ball Mama is holding here next week," said Aleksei. "You'll never make it through the evening with those delightful body-hugging sheaths such as you have on tonight. I suggest you each wear a tent."

"But, darling, it is a tradition," said Katrina. On Russian Easter, we must have all the proper foods. Emma dear, you will attend, of course."

"When is this ball?" I asked.

"Sunday. It will be quite a gala occasion."

"All the nobility will be there," said Oleg. "They will be coming from all over Europe. It's not often they get a chance to wear all their ribbons and decorations and mingle with, as they put it, their own kind."

"They're a bunch of pathetic mediocrities who still have a sense of totally undeserved entitlement," Irina scoffed. "They have spent their lives hoping the people will call them back."

"It happened with Juan Carlos in Spain," said Katrina.

Irina laughed. "That country is not even a quarter

the size of Russia and the monarchy was reinstated by Franco. Could you imagine what would happen if Yeltsin announced that he wished to be succeeded by the House of Romanov?''

Dmitri struggled to his feet. "I really must go," he said, walking over to his hosts. "I have early practice tomorrow. I have enjoyed the evening immensely and I thank you so much for inviting me." As he walked out he turned to me. "I will see you tomorrow, Emma."

Aleksei walked over and sat down beside me. "You are interested in skating, Emma—or is it skaters?" he asked with a sardonic smile.

I looked at him coolly. "To that question I have two answers and one question. I am always interested in viewing art and artistry. I am not a teenage groupie. And why should this concern you?"

He took my hand, "You concern me, Emma, more than any woman I have ever met."

I could see that this was not the fatuous statement of a glib Casanova. He was dead serious. This might present a complication or a convenience, I wasn't sure which at the moment.

"I am taking Irina to the Kirov Ballet tomorrow night. Will you join us, please?" he asked. "It is a very special night—the eight hundredth performance of *Sleeping Beauty*, the wonderful ballet Petipas created together with Tschaikowsky."

"I'd be delighted."

We heard loud voices at the other side of the room.

"But how can you accept the gangsterism that is going on in St. Petersburg?" It was Irina, almost

Cynthia Smith

shouting at Prince Oleg and his brother. "The shoot-
ings, the murders. Is this any better than the terror
and fear we lived with under communism?"

Prince Mikhail shrugged. "Under the old regime,
everyone was threatened and in danger. Now it is only
those who do business with the Mafia. If one chooses
to mix with criminals, one must be ready to accept
the consequences."

"You make it sound as though those who deal with
them have a choice," argued Irina. "Remember when
the Nevsky Palace, our best hotel, refused to meet a
gruoppirovka's demands for monthly 'protection'
payments? The next day a man came in with a Ka-
lashnikov and machine-gunned the bar, killing tourists and Russians. It was found that the hotel's
security TV cameras had been mysteriously turned
off. Now the Nevsky and all the other hotels are paying. And did the police do anything about it? Of
course not. They're owned and supported by the Mafia."

"My dear, I believe you are exaggerating," said
Oleg placatingly. "And you are giving our guest a
very bad image of our country."

"It's hardly news to anyone in the world who reads
a newspaper," Irina continued scathingly. "Weren't
you just a trifle upset when Vice-Governor Manevich
was assassinated?" she continued. "Various government agencies have suggested that his death was due
to his attempts to stifle corruption in high places—
and that certain powerful people have a vested interest in seeing that the murder is never solved. And how
about the whole country's favorite TV anchorman?

He thought he was powerful enough to speak out against the Mafia and was shot dead as he was inserting his key into his front door. That doesn't bother you?''

Aleksei walked over to Irina and put his arm around her. "*Krasavitza moya,* there's no point to this. You won't change them, nor they you. Besides, what would you have them do?''

Her eyes were blazing. "Speak up! They are not poor powerless peasants or workers. They are wealthy men of some power. Let them be heard so that this lawlessness is stopped.''

"Money and power, unfortunately, do not stop bullets, as you just indicated,'' he said. "Remember, too, that members of the royal family are not particularly welcome in Russia. Here we are in a grand home filled with precious art our ancestors were lucky and wily enough to smuggle out of the country when they escaped, much of which the Russian people believe belongs to them. Do we really want to call attention to ourselves?''

I was dying to jump in and help Irina, but I was a guest in this house and it would have been wrong of me to attack my hosts and their way of life. I wanted to point out that those who stand by in silence when they see injustice done are as guilty as the perpetrators.

"Sadly, we Russians have a bloody history of executions of those we do not like at the moment,'' continued Aleksei. "The terrorists who killed Czar Alexander II, the Cossacks who led pogroms, the Bolsheviks who shot the royal family, Stalin, who murdered millions. Our family has been in exile for a long time and we are thrilled to have been able to return. Russia is part of us, it is our motherland. To take any public position right now would be foolish and extremely risky. Things will change, I assure you. Be patient, our time will come. But right now we must not, as the Americans say, rock the boat. Do you understand that, Irinitchka?''

She looked at him stonily, her eyes filled with tears, and walked out of the room.

Sometimes it's hard to be young. I remember my battles when I was in my twenties. Unfortunately, my generation had no major causes—the Vietnam War was over, affirmative action was making inroads in eliminating racism, although there's still a long way to go, *Roe* v. *Wade* is still holding, and the title Ms. is an accepted part of the language. But the need to battle authority burns in the breast of any young person who's worth his or her salt. So parents were forced to take the heavy hit because they were the closest authorities to attack. My rebellion took the form of sleeping with a string of young men my mom and dad regarded as unsuitable. In retrospect, they weren't unsuitable, they were despicable, grungy, self-involved, antifeminist dickheads who engaged in the adolescent sophistry of claiming that anyone who made money was an enemy of mankind. But Irina had real cause. She and all young Russians felt betrayed and they had every right to be angry. No, furious.

IV

DMITRI'S BMW GOT us to Lomonosov in no time at all. It's only twenty-five miles north of St. Petersburg and the fairly empty roads made easy going. We pulled up in front of a group of buildings that looked dark and deserted.

"The Tsvetnuye Metalluy Company," he said sarcastically, gesturing grandly.

I was stunned. "But there's no one here," I said.

"Oh yes, many people are inside working in the bigger building. The small one is the skating rink."

"But it seems dark—there are no lights on."

He smiled sourly. "Most likely the power-plant workers quit again because they have not gotten paid for months. This is not unusual."

"How do they see to work?"

"Like how we see to skate. By natural light. In the

summer months when we have the white nights, it is O.K. But this time of year, it is gray skies, so it is a little more difficult.'' He shrugged. "In today's Russia, one deals with what one has. Let me tell you a joke that is going around.

"Boris arrived in hell and was told he had a decision to make—to go either to capitalist or communist hell. He wanted to compare them, so he wandered over to capitalist hell and asked the first person he met, 'What's it like here?'

'' 'Well, in capitalist hell, they flay you, boil you in oil, chain you to a rock, and slash you with sharp knives.'

'' 'That's terrible,' gasped Boris. 'I'm going to check on communist hell.'

"There he discovered a long line waiting to get in. He pushed his way to the head of the line, where he found Karl Marx busily signing in people. Boris asked what communist hell was like.

'' 'In communist hell,' said Marx, 'they flay you, boil you in oil, chain you to a rock, and slash you with knives.'

'' 'But that's exactly the same as capitalist hell!' protested Boris.

'' 'True.' Marx, sighed. 'But most of the time we're out of oil, chains, and knives.' ''

He took his bag out of the car and we walked toward the rink. As we entered we saw a few skaters on the ice busily doing figures. As we walked the dark corridor leading to the dressing rooms, a number of people greeted him. He asked one of them how the ice was and got a so-so gesture. Dmitri pointed me to the entrance to the arena stands.

"You sit there. You will see me soon."

He was glorious to watch as he whirled around the arena. After about a half hour he came over to me.

"You're fantastic, Dmitri."

He smiled. "Thank you, but there are others equally good, if not better. It is important that I work for some hours. Will you find how to occupy yourself during that time?"

You bet. "No problem, Dmitri. I'll just wander around the place and walk into town. As I told you, I just must get to the science museum. What time should I be back?"

"I should be finished by three," he said.

Me, too, I thought.

I stood outside the factory and looked up. How they got any light in there was a miracle. Almost half of the windows were broken and covered with irregularly cut pieces of cardboard and the remaining half were opaque with what looked like years of accumulated dirt. The whole thing typified the paradox of Russia and Russians. How could a country that produced such great artists have a population so unconcerned with aesthetics? I have known many Russians, and they have an "it's good enough" attitude toward everything. Their homes look like Salvation Army showrooms; as long as it functions even minimally, no one really cares what it looks like. Some attribute this tendency to necessity, the result of shortages under communism. But it has nothing to do with availability, only attitude. Some blame lack of money for their lack of concern with style. Then how come Mrs. Khrushchev and Mrs. Brezhnev, who were rolling in rubles, looked like they just stepped out of the Sears plus-sizes department? Have you ever heard of a Russian furniture designer? Or fashion designer? Raisa Gorbachev caused an international stir because she was the first well-dressed, stylish Russian woman the world has seen since Catherine the Great. I looked up again at the factory. At least wash the damned windows, I thought.

I pulled the door open with difficulty; it was hanging on its hinges. I peeked in and saw a receptionist who was doing what receptionists the world over do— she was painting her fingernails. I retreated and looked at my watch; it was ten-thirty. Time for coffee or tea break. Sure enough, within minutes, the door opened and people streamed out. It was a balmy day and they sat around on rocks and the ground sipping jars of tea and munching on things from their paper bags. Having observed the local style of dress when coming in from the airport, I had dressed to pass for a native: I wore black pants, black jacket, carried a shopping bag, and looked unhappy. I noticed a young woman sitting by herself on a tree stump and walked over to her and sat down. We got into conversation and she told me she had been working there for over a year. She said it seemed wonderful when it first opened; everything inside was new and shiny. She heard the owners had bought all the machinery from a big Japanese company. But slowly, things began to break down. Apparently, the Japanese had passed off old models of everything, and supplied no repair parts. As a result, when something broke down, it stayed that way. When the whistle blew to return, I walked in with her.

The so-called factory was an incredible fiasco. Half of the machinery stood idle, obviously in a state of disrepair. Workers were talking, smoking, and wandering around. There was an air of disinterest and an obvious total lack of supervision. I had to watch my way carefully because the concrete floors had large potholes every few feet. I didn't have to worry about being stopped by a manager; if there were any such individuals, they were permanently off duty.

I went outside and walked around the building to the back. Walls were cracked, garbage was piled up.

"Hey, who are you?" I heard someone yell in Russian. Two men had come around the building and were looking at me very unpleasantly.

I smiled. "I'm sorry—I don't speak Russian."

"What are you doing here?" said the one who had yelled. He still spoke Russian. He was big, wide rather than tall. He had pitted skin, and the bulging arms and neck of a man who works out regularly, plus another bulge where there shouldn't be that was apparently a gun.

The second man spoke English with a heavy accent. "This is private property."

He was very expensively dressed, but no amount of tailoring could hide the rolls of flesh and gut. One of his eyes seemed to be heavy-lidded and was half-shut, which gave him a very sinister look. The way the other man reacted to him, it was apparent he was the senior of the duo. I noticed a very large Mercedes parked on the side of the building.

I looked properly chastised. "I was with my friend, who is skating next door, and I got tired of watching him, so I came out for a walk. What is this place?" I asked ingenuously.

"It is a factory. You have no business here."

I looked suitably remorseful. I started to walk away. "I'm sorry, I didn't know."

They stood there watching until I reached the rink. I looked back as I opened the door of the rink building and they were still watching. I went inside and took a seat in the stands. I must admit I was a bit shaken. I had just met my first mafiosi.

I was quiet in the car on the way home and Dmitri noticed.

"Did you not like Lomonosov?" he asked.

"Everything was lovely."

"You look so sad, you could be Russian."

"I'm not sad, just serious. I had a peculiar incident at the factory next door to your rink." I told him about meeting the men.

Now he looked serious. "The Mafia. I fear they have much to do with the plant. I have seen them around there often. It used to be such a happy, busy place. They suck the blood out of everything," he said angrily.

I lapsed into silence as we sped—and I mean sped—home. Dmitri was going around eighty miles an hour.

"Aren't you afraid of getting a speeding ticket?" I asked.

He laughed. "*Nyet.* I make this trip often and the police along the way have been paid handsomely to close their eyes when I fly by."

"So this is what the new Russians call a 'free society,' " I said. "You're free to do anything you damned please as long as you have the money to pay for it."

"As you Americans say, Emma—you got it."

He dropped me off in front of the house and refused my invitation to come in for *chai.* I was glad because I wanted to think.

"Had a nice day?" asked Aleksei, who was coming down the stairs as I entered the hall. There was no sarcasm; he was obviously trying to be pleasant to make up for his churlish behavior earlier.

"Lovely," I answered.

"Dinner will be at six tonight so that we can make the eight o'clock curtain at the Kirov."

"Fine."

He looked slightly taken aback by the brevity of my responses, but I rushed past him up the stairs before he had a chance to quiz me. I had a lot to think about and didn't have time for chitchat. Nor did I wish to expose myself to his keenly probing eyes and mind.

Dinner was a sensibly light one. It had better have been or I might not have made it into my gown. One is expected to dress respectably for Russian performances. The mixed-bag ragtag look of a New York City Ballet audience is not acceptable here. However, it is a poor country and ostentatious splendor would be in poor taste. So I chose a simple Mayela clinging silk column of tonal shades of chocolate with black. The dress cost me $2,600, which is almost three times the average yearly salary here, but its stark simplicity makes its price indiscernible to any but clothes cognoscenti. Which included Aleksei, of course. He eyed the dress—and me—approvingly. Irina looked absolutely stunning in an equally simple deep purple silk Dior that cost a pretty pack of rubles.

The Mariinsky Theater has the old-world magnificence of all old European opera houses, where everything is gold—from the decorated domed ceiling to the parterre boxes. Huge glittering crystal chandeliers stud the ceiling and the entire theater is a place of enchantment.

Ballet and opera are the only performance arts that always move me. If theater doesn't have superb actors, who speak to the audience rather than to each other so that the audience can hear brilliant words penned by a talented playwright, then I'm apt to spend at least the first act struggling to keep my eyes open. But in ballet and opera, the music, movement, and voices capture me at the outset and keep me rapt throughout.

The Kirov Ballet company has lost a steady stream of stars to the United States. The fact that they were still able to put on such a marvelous *Sleeping Beauty* was a tribute to the unquestionably superb Russian training. The great ballet we enjoy in the United States owes a tremendous debt to the Russians, who gave us Ballanchine, Baryshnikov, Nureyev, Makarova. Fokine, Pavlova, and Nijinsky created a tradition that set the standard throughout the world.

The pleasure of a wonderful performance was enhanced by the loudly appreciative response of the audience. It's always more exciting when everyone shares your enthusiasm. The wild applause after a particularly beautiful pas de deux was truly exhilarating. The Russians take their music and ballet seriously, especially in St. Petersburg, which has a long history as the culture capital of the nation.

Every seat was taken, which meant the lobby during intermission was jammed. The three of us stood together eagerly discussing the specific intricacies of the ballet. We were on such a high that we barely noticed the jostling. Irina was talking with sparkling eyes about a young ballerina who was making her debut that evening.

"We are very proud of our ballet, Emma. We Russians consider it a national treasure. Unfortunately, it is no longer affordable by the people. Under the old regime, the state would send buses into the country to bring farmers and workers to the theater. Today, you'll see only the new Russians and Mafia and tourists. They are the only ones who have the money."

"True, the Communists loved the ballet," said Aleksei. "They supported it because it was a distraction from reality; it took the people's minds off the misery of their lives. The people loved it for the same reason. And also because it is an art without speech, which meant they could enjoy the entertainment without being harangued by the endless preaching. If you like, we can go backstage afterward and visit with my old friend Oleg Vinogradov. He has been the director of the Kirov for over twenty years."

"He'll tell you how wonderful it was for him under the old regime," said Irina. "He got all the money he needed because the government supported the arts. The expense of mounting a new ballet was no problem—all he had to do was ask. Today they are struggling for every ruble."

Suddenly she turned around for a second and then seemed to crumble. Aleksei caught her before she hit the floor. The crowd was so noisy that no one seemed to notice.

"Mn'e nuzhna pomasch—doktar." I need help, a doctor, yelled Aleksei. The crowd started to quiet down as people realized something was amiss.

A woman pushed her way forward. "I am a doctor." She dropped to the floor and immediately felt for Irina's pulse. She looked shocked and began to administer CPR. I stood there helplessly. A man who was apparently the manager suddenly appeared and began to tell everyone to give us room. This was a people who were used to following orders, and everyone moved back within seconds. In the U.S., you'd need an animal prod to get the rubberneckers to alter their positions. After a number of minutes the doctor looked up and shook her head.

"You mean she's dead?" I said incredulously. I felt my eyes fill with tears.

Aleksei looked stunned. "But she's only twenty-eight," he said. "She couldn't have had a heart attack."

"We'll have to do an autopsy," the doctor said. "The police must be called at once."

"Carry her to my office," said the manager. As he

and another man carried Irina, Aleksei whipped out his cellular phone and spoke rapidly into it. Within five minutes police arrived with ambulance attendants. I looked at Aleksei speculatively. Who did he phone to get such speedy action?

We went home to tell his parents, who would call Irina's family. I went to bed early but couldn't sleep. I finally gave up at three-thirty and went down to the kitchen. I found Aleksei sitting at the round wooden table with a hot drink.

He looked up at me. "Would you like a *gogl mogl*? Mother used to make it for us when we were sick, or sad. Russians get sad a great deal of the time; we are not a happy people. The drink is just tea, honey, and cognac, although I understand every family has its own version. Would you like me to make you some?"

I nodded and shortly we were both staring into our drinks.

"It wasn't a heart attack," he said quietly.

"How do you know?"

"I was called by the medical examiner with the results of the autopsy. She was stabbed to death in the heart."

I stared at him. "But there was no wound, no blood."

"It was a stiletto. A very sharp wafer-thin blade causes practically no exterior bleeding. It's all inside."

"But the doctor saw no wound."

"With such a weapon," he said, "it is very difficult to find the wound. The victim dies almost at once

61

and the edges of the wound compress immediately until it is virtually invisible.''

I thought for a moment. ''Someone must have tapped her on the shoulder to get her to turn around when she was talking to us.''

''Yes. I remember.''

''But why? Why would anyone want to kill Irina? Was she involved in any revolutionary or dangerous activity? From the way she spoke, she was an activist.''

He shook his head. ''I doubt it. Irina and I were both only children, so we sort of grew up together. I looked upon her as my little sister. She was always burning with indignation about issues. But like many young idealists, she was big on words but very little on action. She sympathized with protests but never attended them. She was terrified of pain. I remember when we were children, the approach of a bee or wasp would cause hysteria.'' His eyes filled with tears. ''Poor Irinitchka, that she should die violently is like some ironic punishment from God.''

He began to cry quietly. I put my arms around him. Sometimes there is nothing to be said and a hug is the only answer.

''She always had strong opinions on everything. I remember her parents' despair when she flatly refused to go to a well-known girls' school in Switzerland. 'I do not want to learn how to pour tea and open bazaars,' she told them. Since sending her to a neighborhood school was out of the question, she ended up being taught by tutors, whom she drove crazy.''

''If her behavior in your home was an example,

she was not one to keep her opinions to herself. Whose toes could she have stepped on?" I asked.

He looked astonished. "But who would care about the ideas of an ordinary young woman?"

I smiled at him sweetly. "Why are your words so familiar, Aleksei? Oh yes, I think they said the same thing about Florence Nightingale, Clara Barton, and Susan B. Anthony."

He smiled sheepishly. "I am sorry. That did sound like what I believe they used to call a male chauvinist pig."

"Irina seemed to be championing the cause of a return to communism," I said. "She apparently felt the people were better off before and are being victimized now."

"Unfortunately, she is not alone. There is a sizable communist party that is trying to regain power."

"Could she have been an active member?"

He shrugged. "Who knows? As you heard her say, she no longer told me everything."

"Cui doesn't bono—who doesn't benefit if the old regime returns?" I asked. "Certainly the Mafia has deeply vested interests in maintaining the status quo. If Irina was any kind of a power in the party, she would pose a threat to them."

"Little Irinitchka? I can't see her achieving sufficient importance to cause fear in anyone."

"Familiarity breeds disrespect. I'll bet every parent whose kid becomes president marvels at how anyone would pay attention to that bigmouthed brat they used to diaper. Irina was intelligent, eloquent, and beautiful—qualities that can be very persuasive. I'd like to find out about her political activities. Do you know any of her friends?''

He thought for a moment. "Yes. Galina Kodorofsky and Genek Sobchak. They were old friends from university days.''

"How about lovers?''

He shook his head. "At the moment, none. Previously, many. She had a long relationship with Shura Petrovnik, which ended a few weeks ago.''

"Did it end badly?'' I asked.

"Well, he didn't want the breakup. But he acceded to her wishes. There were no fireworks to my knowledge. Shura is a pleasant nonviolent type.''

Famous last words. Like the neighbors comment on the boy who slaughters his entire family with a butcher knife. "But he was always such a nice polite boy.''

"Shouldn't we give all this information to the police, Aleksei?''

He laughed. "Surely you jest. They have not solved a murder in years. Even when there are twenty eyewitnesses.''

"Then perhaps you and I should make the effort to find out who killed Irina,'' I said.

"Why? What good will that do? It won't bring Irina back. I'm not a coward, Emma, but I see no purpose in endangering our lives. I don't think Irina would have wanted that.''

I looked at him and said nothing. Usually to the bereaved, finding and punishing the person who killed their loved one brings a sense of closure to a heartbreaking situation. And I didn't think he had a clue

64

as to what Irina would have or have not wanted. He'd obviously never taken her seriously. I wasn't sure he knew or cared for her that deeply. Which hadn't been true of her. I remembered her little exchange with me when she voiced concern over him. Perhaps she was facing up to the reality of who and what he really was. It's tough to find your childhood idol has clay feet.

V

I HEARD KNOCKING on my door. I looked at the clock next to my bed. It was 7:30 A.M.

"Come in," I called.

It was Marushka. She thrust a cordless phone in my hand. Pointing to me, she said, *"Tilifon."*

Shit. Ellis probably tracked me down. I sighed. With his intelligence network, it was only a matter of time. I settled back in bed, ready for an ill-tempered "where the hell have you been?" diatribe—I dislike demanding clients—and said, unenthusiastically, "Hello."

"What's the matter, *ahuvati,* my sweetheart. Did he give a disappointing performance last night? It's all that vodka, I understand it paralyzes the penis, but unfortunately never in the up position."

I smiled happily. It was Abba—my favorite person

in the world, next to my parents. "How did you know where to find me?"

He snorted indignantly. "Do you remember who I am and what I do? For an officer in the Mossad, finding a gorgeous American brunette in Russia is a piece of cake. Especially when one of my men happened to be on the Finnair plane when you flew from Helsinki to St. Petersburg the other day."

"How did he know me?"

"Questions, questions. O.K. I have a picture of you and me on my desk. It confirms my supreme machismo status in the office."

I felt so relieved to talk to him that I nearly cried. You're shocked, I know. I'm supposed to maintain invincible cool in any situation—like a guy. But maybe little boys would have an easier time growing up if they knew it was O.K. to feel and show emotion. Can you imagine how many lives it might have changed if they had let Humphrey Bogart shed just a few tears when Ingrid Bergman flew off with Paul Henreid in *Casablanca*?

Abba and I have been friends for many years. We have helped each other out in various tough and ticklish situations and have become indispensable to each other. His work is dangerous and draining and he rests up in any of my three homes whenever he needs it— my flat in London or apartment in New York when he craves excitement and luxury, my villa in Vila do Mar on the southern coast of Portugal when he wants rest and rehabilitation. We love each other dearly, but there's nothing sexual in our relationship—at least, not on my part. Abba is five feet-six inches, weighs

250 pounds, and is heavily bearded. He looks like a cuddly teddy bear until you notice his eyes—the intelligence and compassion that are usually there, and the calculating coldness when it's required. I never discuss my cases or ask advice or help from anyone. Except Abba. Besides his sagacity, he's a rock of reliability and discretion. I work strictly solo—except for Abba, which enables me to guarantee total secrecy. The more people you work with, the more leaks are created. Most of my clients are of the level of prominence that attracts the media. Besides guaranteed success, what my clients most prize is total discretion.

"I'm flattered that you went through all that trouble to find me," I said in a light voice. "Is this a 'so what's new?' call or are you just looking for someone to talk to?"

"What's wrong, Emma?" he asked quickly.

"What makes you think something's wrong?"

"Listen, *tsotskele,* I have a psych degree from Brooklyn College and a job in which evaluating a person's tone of voice could mean life or death. Besides, you'd never end on a preposition unless you're in deep shit. So what's going on? Who's the client and what are you doing for him that's obviously giving you *tsuras*?"

I told him everything.

He whistled. "Ellis Brannock—you're operating in the big time now, honey. I'm impressed." He was silent for a minute. "Those men at the factory—describe the one who spoke English."

69

When I mentioned the drooping eyelid, I heard him gasp.

"Vladimir Nickonov. Speaking of the big time, sweetie, you hit one of the top ten *kus-amacks* of all time. That motherfucker has a bloody history that would make Attila the Hun look like a Boy Scout."

"Who is he?"

"He used to be one of the best the KGB had to offer. And the best were rated by ruthlessness, craftiness, and cruelty. We figured dear old Vladimir would find his niche in some sort of job that would use his special talents. And he did. He is part of the Lomonosov *gruoppirovka.*"

"What's that?"

"Mafia. Let me give you a short lesson in Russian Mafia. They're independent organizations known as *gruoppirovkas*, each one run by a leader called the *autoritet.* The name Mafia has been applied to them because of their Sicilian-like interests in crime of all kinds—drugs, prostitution, and the protection racket, which they gave the Russian word *kruysha,* which means 'roof' to convey total coverage of the business they're so-called protecting. Anyone who starts a business, once it becomes profitable, gets a visit from one of the *gruoppirovkas* and is told he has a new partner. An accountant is sent in to examine the books and figure how much the business can pay for 'protection' without crippling its operation, which they now have an interest in keeping profitable. Some of the bigger *gruoppirovkas* are even involved in start-ups. They'll finance a new business if someone comes to them with a good idea and no capital. They call it 'stuffing the pig'—you know, like force-feeding a Strasbourg goose to ensure nice rich pâté after you kill it. Deal with them and you've made a Faustian bargain; once they become your partner, it's an arrangement that ends only by death. Yours.''

"What's the Lomonosov?"

"The Sicilian Mafia use family names. The Russians call themselves after the localities in which they started operations.''

"Then Nickonov and his *gruopirrovka* must be a little involved with Ellis's Tsvetnuye Metalluy Company," I said.

"There's no 'little involvement' with Mafia. It's like being a little pregnant. If you saw Vladimir at the factory, he owns it.''

"What do you mean? It's owned by Brannock's foundation.''

"That may be what he thinks, but if the Mafia is there, Brannock is just a silent partner. And that's what he'll be if he makes any moves on the place— silent forever. Those boys don't fuck around; you get in their way and bang, bang, you're dead. Emma, get the hell out of there fast.''

"I can't do that yet, Abba. I have to find out how the Mafia got involved in Ellis's philanthropy. There's something not kosher going on at that board and that's what Ellis is paying me to find out.''

"*Shtuyot*—bullshit. What's the good of all that money if you don't live to enjoy it? You don't even have any heirs to leave it to yet. Say, listen, how about making me your beneficiary? I guarantee it'll go to a good cause.''

"I gave at the office, Abba.''

"Look, *motek,* darling, I don't want to see Nickonov sign you off. He's already seen you."

"He doesn't know who I am. I think he bought my 'innocent intruder' story."

"Maybe for now. But if you continue following up the case, you're bound to come to his attention. Don't underestimate him. He's a foul cocksucker but a shrewd one, who has lived this long because he takes no chances. If he thinks you're in any way in his way, you're gone."

"Thanks for the warning. I'll be especially careful."

"My love, you've gotten yourself into some rough situations before, but they were a day at the beach compared to this one. The Sicilian Mafia at least has some sort of rules and predictability; they kill each other and never harm each other's wives and children. The Russians kill everybody, and often brutally. They're big into teaching lessons like murdering the kids, wives, and parents of someone they want to impress. And anyone who gets in their way just gets popped—casually, like you'd step on a bug. It doesn't matter who or what he or she is; they're totally unconcerned with what effect the murders will have on law enforcement, the government, or public opinion. Why should they? Everyone is in their pockets, or paralyzed with fear of them."

"Abba, you're trying to scare me."

"Fuckin'-A I am. That's my intention, baby. Listen, kiddo—I love you and I don't like you being involved with murders and murderers."

"I am already," I said, and I told him about Irina.

"Describe her," he said brusquely.

I did.

"Beautiful, dark brown hair and eyes, stylish, great body—at the ballet with Prince Aleksei—who does that sound like?" he asked.

I was silent for a minute. "Me?"

"They made a little mistake once; they won't the next time. When's the next plane out of St. Petersburg?" he asked. "Be on it."

Suddenly my bedroom door opened and two uniformed men burst in. "Emma Rhodes, you are under arrest for murder of Irina Mikhailova Romanov."

"What the hell is that?" said Abba.

"It seems the police think they know who killed Irina—me," I said with more calm than I felt.

"Fuckin' Russian bastards. They're up to their old tricks of laying the crime on anyone handy who has no political connections. Looks like I'll be the one on the plane. Stall them as long as you can. I'll be there in a couple of hours." He hung up.

"Get clothes on," said one of the policemen. Both stood very erect. They said something to each other in Russian, assuming I could not understand them. They were deciding who should have the privilege of watching me dress. "You had the last one, that nice plump *blondinka* last week."

No one is getting his rocks off watching me strip, fella, I thought. One of them spoke English—the one who announced my arrest when they entered.

"I will not get dressed while you are in the room."

"Zaprishchyaitsa." Prohibited, he said.

I sat down on the bed and refused to move. Then

I pointed out that the window was too high for me to jump and there was no other exit from the room. They had a heated discussion, which, of course, I understood. The English-speaking one was willing to give me privacy, but the other one was one of those obdurate civil-servant "I only follow orders" types. So I hauled out the heavy artillery: I began to cry. They became confused. It's amazing how a crying woman can throw the toughest man. They argued for a moment and then left the room after warning me that they were both standing outside my door.

I left the shower on for fifteen minutes after I was out of the bathroom and was fully dressed. I sat on a chair for another ten minutes until they started banging on the door. I let them in and indicated they had to wait while I applied my cosmetics. They watched with fascination as I went through the kind of makeup job I had once at Elizabeth Arden when I felt the need for a day of self-indulgence. I took almost an hour and emerged looking like a Barbie doll. When we finally came downstairs, Prince Oleg was pacing up and down in agitation, and the princess ran over to me, looking terribly distressed.

"Emma, my dear, what can we do? This is terrible, all a horrible mistake. First Irina, now this. I cannot bear it. Too much tragedy all at once."

Just then the front door opened and Aleksei came in. When he saw the police, he stopped dead. "What is all this?"

"I'm being arrested for Irina's murder," I said simply.

He turned red with fury and turned on the two policemen. "Idiots!" he barked in an imperious manner. This was the aristocrat landowner speaking to the peasants. "Miss Rhodes is an American who has been in this country for two days and hardly knew Countess Irina. I demand you release her immediately and leave my home at once."

They were a little uncertain of themselves. The doorbell rang and Aleksei opened the door.

"And who might you be?" he asked of the short, heavy man who walked in.

"Sledovatel Ivan Golov," he said, showing an official folder. A detective. The two policemen looked relieved to see him.

"I was a bit delayed." He looked at me. "Miss Rhodes, have my men read you your rights?"

"No. I didn't know you had them in Russia."

He smiled. "Oh yes, we are a free country now."

"Free to make asses of yourselves by arresting someone who couldn't possibly have committed the crime?" asked Aleksei.

"Witnesses tell us Miss Rhodes was standing in exactly the position to wield the knife that killed the victim," said the detective mildly.

"So was I," said Aleksei curtly.

"Not to mention the mobs of people around us," I added.

"No, Prince Aleksei, the witnesses say you were standing facing her, but not next to her. Miss Rhodes was between you."

"That's nonsense. What witnesses?"

"That will all come out in time," said Sledovatel

Golov. "Right now Miss Rhodes must come with us."

"She is not leaving this house until I speak with two of my friends—State Duma Deputy Guzinsky and Police Chief Viktor Kravchenko," said Aleksei firmly. "You will wait in here." He led them into the library. Obviously awed by both the surroundings and the names Aleksei mentioned, they sat down quietly while Aleksei left to make his calls in another room.

Catch Columbo being impressed with Aleksei's performance. He would have merely flicked his cigar ash into his cuff and taken off with the alleged perpetrator—apologetically, of course. For two hours the men sat there patiently. Waiting is an ingrained part of Russian life. Incredible. I was getting antsy. Where the hell are those callbacks? But they sat calmly, as though they wouldn't move until they were given permission. Aleksei kept going out and returning. Marushka brought in tea, which they took gratefully, looking totally uncomfortable with the delicate china.

We heard the doorbell ring and a maid came in and looked at me. "Colonel Levitar."

Abba came striding into the room and I ran over and threw my arms around him.

"My hero—am I glad to see you," I whispered into his ear.

"I know. I left my white horse double-parked outside."

I introduced him and they were obviously impressed by his entrance; he cut quite a figure in his Israeli Army uniform. He took the hat off, but not until he was sure they had noticed the bullet holes in it. Aleksei's eyebrows went up when Abba spoke to them in perfect Russian. Abba had one of those rare ears for language that enabled him to sound like a native. It's not just knowing the words and grammar, it's a matter of being able to hear and reproduce the right musical cadences.

He also had the instinct to recognize instantly who to deal with and what button to press.

"Sledovatel Golov—could I speak to you privately for a moment?"

They left the room and I could see Aleksei was disconcerted. They came back within fifteen minutes and the detective said to his men, "*Idyiti*—let's go."

They arose obediently, showing no surprise.

He turned to me. "We will notify you if we need you for a witness when we find the culprit."

And they left.

I sank back into my chair, stunned. I looked at Aleksei, who looked angry.

"What did you do, Abba?" I asked, mystified.

"You owe me five hundred dollars," he said with a smug smile.

"You mean you paid them?"

"Fuckin'-A. I gave five bills to the top guy and told him three hundred for him and one hundred for each of his men. They'll be lucky if they get fifty."

"And they took it, just like that?"

He looked at me in surprise. "But of course. Three hundred bucks is three months' salary for the detective. I offered him two, but he told me three hundred is the going rate for murder suspects."

"I know there's police corruption here, but I didn't

realize it was that blatant. It's like bargaining to buy a car.''

"Sort of. But you don't get to kick the tires. What's the big deal, *ahuvati,* my darling? He'll just go out and find himself another alleged perpetrator and eventually the murder will join the thousands of other unsolved cases on their books.''

Aleksei was furious. "It's shameful. Russian law and order—it's a joke!''

The prince and princess came in. "Marushka tells us the police have gone and you are still here. What's happened?'' Oleg asked me anxiously. He looked at Abba. "And who is this fine military gentleman?''

"This is my friend Colonel Abba Levitar of Israel. He came here to help me—and he did. I'm free and no longer under suspicion.''

Neither he nor the princess asked any questions. No one asks how anything gets done in Russia. What's the point? They don't expect to hear the truth, and I'm not sure they want to know.

"Come, children, it is time for breakfast," said Katrina happily. "And I think we might have champagne with our juice this morning. I believe we all need it.''

We sat down at the table. As always, within minutes everyone was charmed with Abba. He plunged into the food with the gusto that makes all cooks and hostesses adore him. When Raya asked him what kind of eggs he preferred, and would he like potatoes, he looked at her pleadingly and asked, "Could I possibly have kasha instead?''

Her wrinkled face broke into the biggest smile I had ever seen on her. *"Da, da."*

When he took the first taste of that ubiquitous Russian side dish, he looked up at her. "Mmm, this is as delicious as the kasha my grandmother used to make." I thought she would burst with joy; she left the room laughing.

"You certainly have a way with servants," said Prince Oleg with a smile.

"With princesses, too," said Katrina, patting Abba's hand. "Do you have a hotel, Abba?"

"Not yet," he said. "I came straight here from the airport."

"Good, then you must stay with us."

"If you're sure it's no trouble."

"Nonsense," said the prince. "We have plenty of room. You've come to help Emma and you must stay close to her, then."

Aleksei's face darkened.

I had told them nothing about Ellis's case. After breakfast, I took Abba up to his room and sat with him while he unpacked. I told him about Aleksei's little drama and the calls that never came.

"He probably never phoned at all. Either he doesn't really know those big honchos or he does and doesn't want to bother them."

"Then what was the whole act about?"

He shrugged. "To impress you. To show you what a big man he is. To make you think he really cares."

"Or maybe he really doesn't want me to get off," I said thoughtfully. "What do I really know about

Aleksei—other than he's handsome and rich—but how did he get rich?''

"In today's Russia, that's easy. But right now we have an appointment,'' he said as he took his shirt and pants off unselfconsciously and put on black trousers and a black shirt.

"I see you know the national costume,'' I said. "Everybody warned me not to dress like a tourist to avoid being singled out by roving Gypsies or others who are supposed to prey upon the innocents. I was also told to keep my dollars in a money belt. The first day here, I could spot tourists in seconds; they're the ones with the suspicious bulges around their waists.'' I stood up. "I'd better get into my basic black, too. Who are we going to meet?''

"A friend of mine. He's a professor of economics and computer science at St. Petersburg University. The guy made up a database of the *gruoppirovkas,* can you beat that?''

"How did he get the data?''

"From a friend of his—one of the Mafia. He'll be there, too.''

"Where are we meeting?''

"On the Nevsky Prospekt, where else?''

"Let's walk it, Abba. That's the only way to really see a city.''

THE NEVSKY PROSPEKT is the heart of St. Petersburg. If you tell a cabdriver you want to go to the center of town, he'll take you to the Nevsky, as it is called. It's over two miles long and has streams of traffic, on the sidewalks and in the streets, all hours of the day and night. Lined with shops, banks, restaurants, and offices, it's Main Street, Times Square, and Fifth Avenue all in one. As you stroll along, you see crowds of laughing young people, who, like the young all over, are enjoying now and not worrying about the future. The old women, who are probably not that old, dressed drably and carrying worn tote bags, and old men in shabby clothes smoking cigarettes, look sad and joyless as they remember a bleak past and look ahead to a hopeless future. Turn your head left or right and there are picturesque canals with little bridges offering softening respites from the hustle and bustle of the Nevsky. Look down the Griboyedev Canal and prepare to be stunned by a fairy-tale apparition—the Church of the Resurrection, also known as the Savior on the Blood, because here is where Alexander II was assassinated by terrorists. Instead of the heavily imposing ecclesiastical architecture we are used to, this church looks like it was designed by Disney. It's fun . . . all red and blue and gold, with five domes.

As Abba and I strolled along we passed small coffee shops where you get a drink and snack at the counter and bring it to a table, you are free to join anyone who is already seated. There are kiosks where people cluster, chatting heatedly, buying beer and snacks. Every block or so is a stand that sells maps and books. Suddenly Abba stopped in front of a store.

"Aha—caviar. Let's go in."

It was a fish store with the wonderful aroma of smoked fish and fresh fish. The place was bustling with activity, clerks running back and forth to fill orders for housewives who were pushing each other out of the way. Politeness has been a casualty of the Russians' daily struggle for survival.

"Look at these prices, Abba. Who can afford to buy here?"

"The 'new Russians,' they're called," said Abba. "The ones who make big rubles stock-trading."

"Stocks? I thought all the companies were in hock up to their eyeballs? What can their stock be worth?"

"It's complicated. Nobody pays their debts; every company owes every other company. So they give each other IOUs—and that's what they trade and pay each other. They're called *veksels*. Company A needs natural gas? They buy it from the gas company with *veksels*. The gas company needs tires for its fleet of trucks? They buy it from Company B and pay with the *veksels* they received from Company A. Last year Almazy Rossii-Sakha, the government-owned producer of nearly one third of the world's diamonds, was negotiating a lucrative contract with De Beers. They haggled for over a year, which almost drained Almazy of cash. No problem—the company just issued over a hundred million dollars in IOUs and kept paying all their bills with them. Creditors accepted them greedily on the speculation that a De Beers merger would bring in big bucks. Sure enough, when news got out that the two companies were due to settle within the month, the Almazy *veksels* went through the roof. They became so hot, you couldn't buy them. People who had bought them early on eventually made sixty five percent profit on their purchases."

I shook my head. The stock market and investing are areas in which I never tread. I don't understand the whole subject and it doesn't interest me. All my money is in mutual funds, treasury bonds, and real estate. I figure the guys running the funds know their business or they wouldn't be in those positions of tremendous responsibility. Unless I'm ready to study the subject and follow the market to become as knowledgeable as they, I'll let them handle it.

Abba bought two five-hundred-gram jars of Mallesol caviar at fifty dollars each, and two cans of red caviar, salmon roe, for sixteen dollars each. "They make nice gifts," he said apologetically to explain his extravagance.

I laughed. "Right. If they ever make it home." A loaf of white bread and a bottle of chilled vodka and Abba would polish it all off within an hour.

Abba asked for his purchases to be wrapped and the saleswoman looked at him as though he were asking for a free herring. She tore off a ragged piece of paper from a roll under the counter and handed it to Abba.

"Here's your wrapping," and she walked away.

"Obviously, service is their middle name," I said.

A woman standing next to us shrugged. "Russian manners."

"What do you expect?" said Abba as we walked out. "Most likely she hasn't been paid for three months, which doesn't help her disposition, not to mention her so-called lifestyle."

There are many churches along and off the Nevsky. Under communism, they were consigned to other uses. One was a basketball practice hall. Another was a library. Now you hear the banging of hammers as many of them are being restored to their former use and splendor. Since some of them are set back a number of feet, many of the spaces in front have become art-selling areas. I cannot recall ever having seen such an aggregation of paintings ranging from mediocre to just plain awful. How can people who have visited the Hermitage consider this art? Maybe the stuff goes over big with tourists, who tell the folks back home that, hot damn, they bought this *original* painting in Russia.

"Do you know where we're going?" I asked Abba.

"There it is—the Literaturnoye—the Literary Café."

We walked into a pleasant restaurant with white tablecloths and pink napkins. The place was filled. At one table, a group of men in suits were engaged in intense conversation. At another, two couples were listening to Mozart being played by a pianist and violinist in the corner of the room—softly, thank goodness. One thing about Russian restaurants—they almost always feature entertainment. If you've come for the floor show, that's fine. But if you're seeking a nice place to dine graciously and chat quietly, good luck to you. Russian ethnic dances and singing are usually lusty and what the performers lack in ability they make up in sound decibels.

"There they are," said Abba, and we walked to the back where two men were drinking tea.

As we approached their table one of them jumped up with a big smile when he saw Abba and gave him a big hug. "Abba, my good friend." He was a short man in his fifties with a graying mustache and bright brown eyes that noticed me at once. "And this is the lovely Miss Emma you told me about."

"Emma, meet Professor Anatoly Yakolov."

We all have our preconceived cliché visions and mine of a highly respected professor at the eminent St. Petersburg University was rumpled tweeds, a pipe, and a battered leather briefcase. It was a bit of a shock reconciling to a shabby navy-blue zippered golf jacket, plaid cotton shirt with slightly frayed collar, and a black plastic shoulder bag. Oh well, I guess there's a disparity between American and Russian salaries in academia. I didn't know until later how much of a disparity.

He bowed slightly and then turned to the younger man in a black turtleneck and expensive-looking brown suede jacket sitting at the table. Very fair with blue eyes and blond hair, his coloring was Scandinavian but his face was Slavic, with flat planes and high cheekbones.

"This is my friend Stanislaus Chirkasov."

We looked at each other and both liked what we saw.

"Come," said Anatoly. "Join us for *chai*—or would you like something stronger?"

We shook our heads, sat down, and all looked at each other happily.

"Abba tells me you have a complete database on all the *gruoppirovkas*—names, clients, and activities," I said to Anatoly.

He nodded.

"How did you ever get such material?" I asked.

"It's not the kind of information you get from ringing doorbells and making phone calls."

He smiled. "Let us say it required a little help from my friends," he said, looking at Stanislaus.

"I assume all the Mafia groups know you have this information. How do they allow you to live?"

"It is really very simple. I am their Switzerland."

"Switzerland has always been able to stay untouched because the fighting nations needed a neutral spot," said Abba. "During World War II, Germany put all their gold and money there, as did individual Nazis. People and countries at war need a safe house and also a place to hedge their bets."

"Why do you need him?" I asked Stanislaus.

"Our *gruoppirovka* needs to know things about our competition," said Stanislaus. He spoke English perfectly, but with simplistic syntax and somewhat roughly.

"Aren't you afraid he'll supply this data to the police?"

Stanislaus and Anatoly laughed. "Why? What would they do with it if they had it?"

"What do you need to know about your competition and why?" I asked.

"So that we don't waste time trying to take over a business that's already in another *gruoppirovka*'s hands."

"You mean you never approach each other's 'clients'?" I asked skeptically. "Now you're going to tell me that you observe some kind of ethical code and there's honor among thieves, and then you're going to try to sell me the Hermitage."

"Of course not," said Stanislaus. "Matter of fact, we steal from each other all the time. However, we try to determine which of our competitor's clients fit into our operational structure. If not, it may be more cost-effective to look elsewhere."

All of a sudden his English changed.

"Cost-effective." I turned to Abba. "He sounds like a Proctor and Gamble marketing manager. Do you go into 'market share,' too?"

"You think the Mafia are just a bunch of crude ignorant brutes, Emma," said Anatoly. "It may have begun that way, but now, like any business that grows, the level of sophistication has increased and more educated and what you call savvy people have entered the field."

"You call gunning down a government minister and a popular TV personality sophisticated?" I asked.

"Assassination is a tool of our trade," said Stanislaus, "much as it is in Abba's."

"We kill killers," said Abba grimly, "men who have been responsible for mass murders. Not innocent people whose opinions we dislike."

I shook my head. "I can't believe all this. We're talking about crime and destruction as though it were a wholesale plumbing business and this could be a Rotary Club meeting."

Stanislaus sat up and looked angry. "It's easy for you to sit and judge. You're rich, established, and from a stable, well-run country. When we wanted to end the regime of old men who lied to us and had us living in daily fear, the younger generation kicked them out and brought in Gorbachev. He promised us everything, but accomplished nothing. Maybe we were impatient and didn't give him enough chance, but we now knew how the rest of the world lived and wanted our share of the good life quickly. Then we got Yeltsin and his friends. Which means that all we really got was an anarchistic free-for-all with every government official grabbing what he could and the people starving in a land that has enough natural resources to equip the world. It became every man for himself. We had to grab, too, in order to survive.''

I was quiet. "I apologize. You're right. I have no right to judge. But I think I have the right to ask why you started out talking like a third-grade dropout and switched to lecturing like a college professor.''

He smiled. "Just another tool of the trade. Education is not a highly valued commodity in my business. I'm afraid I'm so used to my 'plain man of the people' role that I forget when to switch over.''

Abba summoned the waiter. "How about getting some *pelmeny*?" he asked us. They are tasty little envelopes of boiled dough filled with chopped meat and sautéed onions. Of course, like eighty percent of Russian dishes, they're served with sour cream. We all agreed and soon there was a steaming platter in front of us that we tucked into with relish, and more tea.

After demolishing a good number of the delicacies, Stanislaus asked, "Anatoly tells me you want to know about the Lomonosov *gruoppirovka*. As it happened, we had a *razborka* with them last week. That's a meeting that *gruoppirovkas* have with each other to straighten out difficulties among us.''

"Was Nickonov there?" Abba asked.

Stanislaus's face clouded. "Oh yes. Vladimir was there, of course. A more miserable son of a bitch you never met." He looked at me. "Excuse my language, please. What would you like to know about them? But first, tell me why you want to know."

I had planned to give them my usual cover story— I'm a writer researching a new book. That usually gets me everywhere. It's amazing how much people will tell you if they think it's going into literature. For some, it's the closest thing to Andy Warhol's fifteen minutes of fame. But something told me this guy wouldn't buy it. What the hell, I'll give it a shot.

"I'm a journalist. This is for a story."

He looked at me with a cool smile. "It's a story all right. Now it's your turn to try and sell me the Brooklyn Bridge. Who are you really?"

"How did you know I'm not a journalist?"

"I could tell you I'm highly perceptive or have a gut feeling. But I'm afraid it's nothing as esoteric as that. Before our meeting, I checked you out on the Internet and found no listing for books or articles written by an Emma Rhodes."

Abba shook his head sadly. "Exposed by a computer. The fucking information highway is making it tough for an honest spy or con man to make a living anymore."

"O.K. You're right. I'm not a writer. I'm a private resolver." I figured that would give him pause. And did it ever.

The two men looked at me with total bewilderment. "I know English very well, having spent four years at Cal Tech," said Stanislaus. "But I never heard of a private resolver."

"That's because there are no others," said Abba proudly. "You are looking at the sole owner of the title and profession—Ms. Emma Rhodes."

"What do you resolve?" asked Anatoly curiously.

"Anything for anybody who will pay my fee. I relieve people of serious personal problems."

"So does Stanislaus," said Abba. "He relieves them of the serious problem of living."

"As do you, Abba," he said. "You make a distinction that you kill for a noble cause while the Mafia destroys for ignoble greed. May I submit that the people you kill have their own causes and who are you to determine which of you is just?"

"Are you sure you didn't take your degree at the Jewish Theological Seminary?" asked Abba. "You argue like a Talmudist."

Stanislaus bowed his head. "A fine compliment, indeed, Abba. I thank you. I have tremendous respect for their teachings. Actually, I learned them from my grandfather."

Abba's mouth fell open. "You're Jewish?"

"Is that so impossible to believe?"

"You must be Jewish," I said. "You answered a question with a question."

"I knew it," said Abba triumphantly. "You're so damned smart."

I groaned. "Your bigotry is showing again, Abba." I explained to the men: "Abba believes that Jews have an edge on brains. He tells me about the extraordinary number of Jewish Nobel Prize winners, a number that's way out of proportion to the population.''

"May I ask you a question, Abba?" said Anatoly. "Why do Jewish people always want to know who is Jewish? How many times have I heard one Jew say to another something like, 'Did you know Cary Grant was Jewish?' And the other fellow beams and says, 'No!' "

"Cary Grant?" I said.

"He's one of ours," said Abba. "His mother was Jewish."

"Where did you pick up that piece of questionable information?" I asked.

"In a very reliable publication," he said huffily. "I read it in a *New Yorker* profile."

"But why is that so important to you?" Anatoly persisted.

"Until we came to the United States, we were always an unaccepted people living in unwelcoming lands. It's important to us to prove that we contribute value to their society. Besides, we're just damned proud that one of our people made good."

"I understand. When I was going to Cal Tech," said Stanislaus, "I remember how proud we all were when one of the Russian students won a prize. In a sense, his achievement elevated all of us. We felt he had earned for us greater respect and showed the Americans that we had much to offer."

Anatoly nodded. "I see." Then he turned to me. "Emma, what is it you are doing here, and how can we help you?"

"My client has been funding a small business under the misconception that he is building a company that will aid the Russian economy and provide needed jobs.''

"Ah, like the billionaire philanthropist Soros."

"Soros was going for bigger business, which involved more complex management. He gave up after finding out that his money was going into Mercedes cars and Swiss bank accounts and has now switched his whole policy here. My client was aiming for small business that he felt would be more easily controllable."

Stanislaus smiled sardonically. "And he found, of course, that this was not so. The Russian Mafia are an equal-opportunity group; their interest is never affected by creed, color, or size."

"So I've learned about the Tsvetnuye Metalluy," I said.

"That's the company you're investigating?" he asked.

"You seem surprised. Why?" I asked.

His face closed. "Nothing. Just curious."

I'd have to get back to that later. I obviously hit a nerve, but it's sometimes best to let those things sit for a while. Also I thought I might be able to get more information when we were alone, which I was sure could be arranged.

"I'd like to direct his efforts and money toward creating a solid industry here that could provide better living for thousands of Russians instead of for a small ruthless handful."

Stanislaus looked at me with a sad smile. "I'm impressed with your estimable goal, Emma, but less than certain of its success."

"What I would like to know is just how the Lomonosov *gruoppirovka* operates," I said. "They're the ones who seem to have a death grip on the company."

"Most Mafia groups become specialized. The Lomonosov had been into small bars and cafés, penny-ante stuff. They were not what you would call one of the big-time movers and shakers here. Then suddenly something or someone happened and they got tied up with the Tsvetnuye Mettaluy. But having no interest or expertise in tech stuff, they don't understand that to make a real profit, the business must be developed, and this takes time. Being used to crude quick-buck activities, they are just milking the company and using the money to promote their own kind of enterprises."

"Like what?" I asked.

"Prostitution," he said. "In Helsinki. Where men have money to spend on whores. They have a string of Russian and Estonian girls who operate out of the Lomonosov Mafia's own clubs and are making a fortune."

Ellis would love this. Like many men who live profligate lives, he was very religious, an elder of his church. I couldn't wait to tell him his money was being used to sell fornication. That'll make his day.

"Do you know the names and addresses of their clubs?" I asked.

Abba looked at me. "I hope you're not planning to go undercover, if you'll pardon the expression."

"No—I don't like the hours. But my client is a

tough businessman. Hearsay will not make an acceptable report.''

"Would you like to join me?'' asked Stanislaus. "I'm going to Finland tomorrow. Helsinki and Hanko.''

"Where and what is Hanko?'' I asked.

"It is the southernmost city in Finland, on the Gulf of Finland. It is a famous resort with many beaches.''

"That may be appealing in July, but it's April,'' I said.

"It's also one of the biggest ports for cars. I am going to pick up my new car that is being shipped from Germany. Many Russians go there for that purpose. I fly to Helsinki, take the train to Hanko, pick up my car, and drive it back to St. Petersburg. You are most welcome to join me.''

"I'd love to.'' Then I thought for a moment. "Wait a second. I think Katrina and Oleg were planning to have their big annual Russian Easter ball Sunday.''

"No way they'll hold it now, *motek*,'' said Abba "Not until after the mourning period.''

"Who died?'' asked Anatoly.

"The Countess Irina,'' I said.

"The one who was stabbed at the ballet?'' asked Stanislaus.

"How did you know she was stabbed?'' I asked. "The means of death has not yet been officially disclosed.''

Anatoly smiled ruefully. "It is already in my database.''

"You include murders in your information about the Mafia groups?'' I asked.

"Of course. That's an important part of their activities."

"How do you know which *gruoppirovka* has committed the crime?" asked Abba.

"I am told, eventually."

"How do you know Irina was a Mafia casualty?" I asked.

"I know."

"Which one?" I asked tightly.

"That I do not know—yet."

I sank back into my chair. "My God, what a country."

I arranged to meet Stanislaus at the airport the following morning and Abba and I went back to the prince's house. Dinner that evening was a quiet affair with the prince, princess, and Aleksei looking sad and preoccupied. We had simple Russian food, grilled perch, string beans, and a marvelous potato, smoked salmon, sour cream, and a dill dish of which Abba had three helpings. When I went into the kitchen afterward to get Raya's recipe, she told me to boil and then slice eight medium potatoes to which one adds a half pound of smoked salmon in small pieces, one cup of sour cream, and as much chopped fresh dill as desired plus salt and pepper, mix it all together, and serve warm. She said it is just as delicious cold.

"I'll be going away for a few days," I told them. "To Finland."

Aleksei looked at me sharply. "By yourself?" he asked.

If his parents hadn't been sitting there, I would have told him it was none of his business. However, observing the niceties I owed to my hosts and elders, I answered, "No."

I wasn't going to make it easy for him. Why should I?

"Do I know the man?" he asked curtly.

"Perhaps. But I think all that matters is that I do."

He threw down his napkin and stormed away from the table.

"Please excuse my son," said the prince. "But he is very upset about Irina and he is not himself."

Oh, but he is, I thought. After we left the table and the prince and princess retired to their rooms, Abba and I settled down in the salon.

"The guy's nuts about you and he's jealous," said Abba. "What's the big deal?"

I was fuming. "And you think that entitles him to monitor my movements? Jealousy is flattering," I said, "but possessiveness is a pain in the neck. Especially when we're living under the same roof."

"Relax, *hamoodie*—he hasn't tried to break down your door yet. From that furious look on your face, I think his balls would be in jeopardy if he did. Don't worry about it. Just go off tomorrow and have a good time with young Stanislaus. Just be careful. Remember, you'll be mixing with Mafia."

"Will you be here when I get back?" I asked.

"Maybe."

With Abba, that could mean anything.

VI

I FELL IN love with Helsinki at once, maybe because the sun was shining off the waters of the Baltic Sea and the people were smiling and polite and everything and everyone looked happy, clean, and tidy. Shallow reasons, perhaps, but after days in the depressing ambience of St. Petersburg, where the populace looked sad and shabby, the buildings were beautiful but deteriorating, the parks looked scruffy, and one never felt totally secure, it gave me a lift to be in this busy modern safe city.

Compared with other European capitals, Helsinki is fairly new. Four hundred years ago King Gustav Vasa of Sweden decided to challenge the trade monopoly of the Hanseatic League by luring business away from the Estonian city of Talinn. To do this, he commanded the residents of four Finnish towns to pack up and relocate around the rapids on the River Vantaa and form a new city, which became Helsinki.

Up to 1812, Turku to the west had been the Finnish capital and seat of the national university and culture. The big change in Helsinki's fortune came about when Czar Alexander I decided he wanted a new Finnish capital that would be closer to Russia and selected Helsinki. Then Turku suffered a massive fire, which damaged the university and caused it, too, to move to Helsinki. Another fire helped Helsinki's fortunes along even more. Just before the czar's proclamation took effect, Helsinki had a major fire, which required new construction, enabling the famous architect Carl Ludvig Engel to create buildings that stand today as examples of some of the purest neoclassical designs in the world. Add to these the modern structures by famous contemporary Finnish architects like the central railroad station by Eliel Saarinen, and you have an architecturally diverse and interesting city.

The first thing you're aware of in Helsinki is water. Since the city is built on peninsulas, streets, and avenues curve around bays, arched bridges lead to nearby little islands, and ferries take you to the more remote ones. The waterfronts are bustling with boats of all sizes, from small sailboats to ocean liners. Everyone enjoys walking around the *Kauippatori*, which is the square where the main marketplace is set up on the wharf in the center of town. Small wooden stalls and tables sprawl all over, offering fur pelts, dolls, handmade wooden toys, freshly caught fish, coffee, and doughnuts. Women sit at tables crocheting hats and scarves, which are for sale.

Right past the market is the *Pohjoisesplanadi*. Finnish words are endless, but often in them is something vaguely identifiable in English. If you notice, the last part of the street name just mentioned is *esplanadi*, and that's what it is—an esplanade, a park-like strip with flowers and benches bordered on each side by lovely shops like Arabia, Aarika, Marimekko, and Stockmann's, the largest department store in Finland, a cross between London's Harrods and Marks and Spencer.

A cab took us to the Hotel Grand Marina, which turned out to be a delight. Housed inside what was a nineteenth-century warehouse, it faces the south harbor and gave me a constant view from my room of the huge liners sailing back and forth from Sweden.

"Why don't we get a connecting suite?" asked Stanislaus as we stood at the desk waiting to check in. "It's so much more comfortable."

"Nice try, Stanislaus. By the way, do you have a shorter name? If I'm going to have to say Stanislaus every time I want to talk to you, I'll end up with 'hey you.' "

"My friends call me Stosh," he said. "I believe I can now consider you a friend."

"Absolutely," I said, "but not a close enough friend for adjoining rooms."

He shrugged with a smile. "I have time."

Not in your line of work, fella. In your business, to quote an old retirement-village joke, they don't even buy green bananas.

"Where shall we eat lunch?" he asked.

"I don't know the restaurants here at all," I said. "In this surrounded-by-water city, I'd think fish is a good bet."

"Let's save that for dinner; I know an ideal little place fairly near here. But now, how do you feel about reindeer?"

"Concerned about their future."

He laughed. "Don't worry—there are so many of them in Lapland that it's become necessary to cull the herd."

"Wasn't that the line Hitler used?"

"Are you a vegetarian?" he asked.

"No."

"Where do you think your nice juicy steaks come from?"

"Little white trays covered in Saran," I answered.

"O.K., we'll go to Lapland and I'll tell them to plastic-wrap a piece of meat and show it to you at the table before they cook if for us."

"O.K.—but isn't that a bit far to go for lunch?"

THE CAB DROPPED us in front of a nondescript-looking store with a very small modest sign that said LAPLAND RESTAURANT. But inside came the surprise. All the walls were faced with ancient wood, which I later learned came from Lapland. The tables and chairs were all of wood and the place had a quiet charm. We both had sautéed reindeer, which is reindeer that has been marinated and then stewed and served in the center of a large plate surrounded by an inner ring of mashed potato and an outer ring of crushed lingonberries. It was delicious. Coffee was served in *kouksas,* which are wooden cups hand-carved in Lapland. Conversation never lagged. He was articulate, had a wry sense of humor, and became more and more attractive as the afternoon went on. As we lingered over coffee, his being laced with a shot of *Pohjan Poika Snaps*, I felt it was time to get a little nosy. I've always found the direct question gets the best and fastest results.

"Whatever moved you from Cal Tech in glorious sunny California to the Mafia in gloomy St. Petersburg?" (Did I mention that it rains a lot in St. Petersburg?)

"The short answer," he said, "is no green card. My visa to stay in the States expired when my schooling ended. I'm a graduate engineer. Some of my Russian friends made quick marriages with unsuitable American women to get citizenship. I wasn't willing to do that. So I came back to my home, St. Petersburg."

"And you couldn't find a job," I said.

"Sure. I worked in a factory sweeping floors and never got paid. Then I got another job selling cellular phones. I rarely got paid. This went on for a few years. My friend's uncle was a big shot in a *gruoppirovka* that dealt with technical industries and foreign companies. An engineer who spoke English was a prize to them. They made me an offer I couldn't refuse. I held off as long as I could, but the need to eat is a powerful convincer."

I looked at him silently. "That's how you know so much about the Tsvetnuye Metalluy. Your *gruoppi-*

rovka is planning to take it over. And you're going to be the *autoritet* of the operation."

He smiled. "Would you like some dessert?"

Terrific. A freaking Mafia war is about to break out and I'm smack in the middle. I like excitement, but strictly as a spectator. Something tells me that would be a position I would not be able to maintain when and if hostilities begin. From what I've heard about these little set-tos, not too many were left standing at the end. Well, events can't begin without Stosh since he's apparently the point man for his side. So I might as well enjoy myself and do a little shopping.

I looked at my watch. "It's three o'clock, Stosh. I'd like to pay a visit to a couple of the stores in town."

"All right," said Stosh. "You have three hours. We have reservations at my little fish restaurant at six—and tickets to the opera at eight. They're doing *Boris Godunof.*"

"How did you know I'm mad for opera?" I said delightedly.

"I didn't. I just know that I am and I assume any cultured person of intelligence such as yourself would feel the same way."

"Unfortunately, that may be in Europe. But I can't tell you how many people I know who fit that description and look upon opera as a boring dated form of entertainment and opt for Andrew Lloyd Webber."

"Blasphemy! Comparing *Cats* with *Carmen* is a capital offense where I come from. I hope you like Moussorgsky" he said.

"I've heard *Boris,* but I've never seen it. I understand the new opera house here is stunning.''

"I'll meet you in the hotel lobby at five forty-five," he said.

I walked to the *Pohjoisesplanadi* and headed right for Marimekko. I had bought a Marimekko cotton dress in Sweden ten years ago and still enjoy wearing it. The fabrics last forever and the styles are timeless. I stepped into the shop and a half hour later walked out with a pumpkin-colored sheer wool floor-length dress with an inimitable Marimekko fabric design of vertical slashes of purple going down an accordian-pleated skirt. It cost seven hundred dollars and I thanked heaven for credit cards. Then I walked about four blocks to the famous Kalevala Koru. This is a unique establishment that sells traditional Finnish jewelry in designs dating back to the Iron Age and the days of the Vikings. It offers a collection of hundreds of pieces made by hand in Finland of bronze, silver, and gold. The other unique thing about Kalevala Koru is that is was created by a woman in 1937 and today is owned by five thousand women in the form of a nonprofit organization, the Association of the Women of Kalevala, which distributes its profits to charitable causes. Lest you think it's a boutique of the kind run by former housewives who have been misled by the women's movement to think anyone can start a business, last year's annual sales ran to seventeen million dollars.

I walked in and didn't know where to look first— each piece was intricate and fascinating. I finally chose a string of filigreed balls with three pendants that was the replica of a piece found in Halikko buried in an earthenware jar about eight hundred years ago. The price was $5,000. Don't gasp—it was eighteen-karat solid gold with beautifully handmade detail.

I wore it that evening with my new Marimekko dress.

"You look fantastic," said Stosh when I stepped out of the elevator into the lobby, where he awaited me looking very handsome in a charcoal-gray pin-stripe suit that looked like it had cost something close to my necklace.

The restaurant called Wellamo, which means "Mistress of the Sea," was a short walk from our hotel and down a flight of stairs to the street below. It was the kind of simple place with no pretense that I prefer. I had a huge stack of grilled Baltic herrings that one eats like sardines, bones and all, which is why they're served with boiled potatoes to snare the little tickling bones. I usually skip dessert, but fortunately my new dress was the kind that had give and the ginger ice cream intrigued me. It was well worth the caloric stretch. Studded with chunks of ginger, it left my mouth with a lovely tingling sensation and also ensured that my digestive system wouldn't be uncomfortably overwhelmed by the meal. In case you didn't know it, ginger has a salutory effect on diges-tion and is an old and highly effective remedy for stomach upsets and motion sickness. In fact, I take ginger capsules before I fly or board any moving ve-hicle, including a rocking chair. I got the suggestion from a column by the famous health writer Jane Brody of the *New York Times*. It's no old wives' tale—they work.

The Finnish National Opera Hall, opened in 1993, is a striking contrast to a theater like the Mariinsky in St. Petersburg. Modern, almost austere, it has none of the gilt, glitter, and plush romantic elegance of venerable European opera houses. Yet it's handsome, comfortable, and acoustically fine. But it was the audience that interested me most. *Boris Godunof* is a colorful, dramatic, and violent opera. One scene has the stage filled with angry peasants who are beating a pretender to the throne as the blood pours down his face, while behind them are three hanging bodies. In New York, when such scenes end, the audience roars its approval. And after Boris sings his final aria as he writhes and dies in agony, the applause, I've been told, can be deafening. Here, there was only polite clapping. Stosh and I responded instinctively and shouted "bravo" but quieted down quickly when we noticed we were doing solos.

I turned to the young Finnish man next to me and said, "Isn't this a rather subdued audience? Don't you usually cheer?"

He smiled and said, "Only for Puccini."

Finns are a lovely but laid-back people. They're calm and easygoing. I asked one Finnish woman I knew how she would describe her people and she said, "Honest and modest." That's pretty accurate. The president of the country does not use a special limousine—he rides to his office either on the tram or by bicycle. Chauffeured cars are only for state occasions. You may find it hard to believe, but there is very little if any tipping. The first time a hotel bellman said no to a tip, I panicked, figuring I had suddenly suffered a major hearing loss. When a cabdriver took my credit card, a great convenience, filled in the slip with the exact amount, leaving no room for tip, and then said thank you, I thought of New York. Try to escape from a taxi in Manhattan without leaving the cabbie's concept of a suitable tip and he will probably follow you for blocks hurling loud invectives.

At the opera during intermission I noted tables set up in the lobby bearing numbers; on each one was a plate of pastries, a cup of coffee, and a snifter of cognac. These had been prepaid by specific people before the opera. The intermission crowd milled around, but no one touched anything on a table except for the person who had ordered it. The expectation that people would never take what wasn't theirs seemed to be a given. At one section of the waterfront in Helsinki there is a designated place where locals come to wash their rugs in the sea. They hang them on special lines to dry, but they feel no need to hang around themselves. Some take the opportunity to have coffee in a nearby café, others go home and return later. No one worries about rugs being stolen. As one woman said to me, "Who would bother? We all have the same rugs anyway."

They are a simple, unaffected people who on the whole do not worship wealth or crave possessions. They are stalwart folk who love the simple life and prize primitive living, which they view as winning a battle with the tough elements of dark nights and brutal winters. Every Finn I met had a country house usually located on a cold lake. They go off every weekend, all year round, to their cabins to get away from it all—meaning all the modern conveniences. No electricity, no running water, and no indoor plumbing

When I ask why, the answer is a pitying look. Obviously, I don't get it. They're right. Sure, I could understand the need to schlep water from a well, stagger out to an outhouse in the dead of winter, and chop wood to cook and heat with—if I was doing an anthropological study among the Aleuts. But when you know that all the comforts are just a few hours away, isn't this a self-deluding exercise and you are just playing at self-deprivation?

Then there's the sauna—a national tradition. The sauna is a small wooden building on the edge of the lake where the whole family sits naked, often together, to enjoy 150-degree-dry heat, after which they plunge into the freezing lake. In the winter, they merely cut holes in the ice. Why? They tell me it's a spiritual as well as physical experience. I have never understood the joys and benefits of self-torture or flagellation. Why should suffering or deprivation improve your body or purify your soul? When I ask for a rationale, they look at me sympathetically and I look at them incredulously. Then we shake our heads, smug in the knowledge that the other just doesn't get it. I guess it's something one has to be born to.

We walked out from the opera feeling exhilarated as one does after a thrilling performance. When we got outside, it was a glorious, star-filled night. Stosh suddenly stopped in the middle of the street and threw his arms open to the sky. "It is a beautiful night, the opera was beautiful, you are beautiful." And he drew me into his arms and kissed me. It started out as affection and then became sexual as our mouths opened to receive each other. After a minute or so we drew apart, a bit shaken by the unexpected intensity.

"Our rooms may not be next to each other," he murmured, "but at least they're on the same floor."

I laughed. "Business first, pleasure later. Where is the nightclub that my client is unknowingly subsidizing?"

We walked to the Melodi, which was upstairs in a building on a main thoroughfare The place looked quite elegant. Soft music was supplied by a small orchestra and tables were filled with men and women, drinking and laughing and seeming to have a quiet good time. It looked like a luxurious private club. It was only after a while that you became aware of something odd—the men were of varied ages, going well into the seventies, but the women were all in their twenties.

We sat down and a waiter approached. He wasn't rude, but he sure wasn't welcoming. We ordered drinks; Stosh asked for brandy and I requested white wine.

"They don't encourage men to bring their own women here," he said.

"Apparently. I bet the check will reflect their displeasure."

The waiter was back quickly with the drinks without asking if we wanted anything else, and put the bill on the table. Hello and good-bye. Stosh looked at it and whistled.

"Skolka?" I asked.

"In dollars—fifty."

We finished our drinks quietly, just looking around. "Time flies when you're having fun," I said. "I've seen enough. Let's get out of here."

We started to get up when a man approached our table.

"Dobry vechir, Stosh." It was the man I had seen with Nickonov at the factory in Lomonosov.

"And a good evening to you, Yury," said Stosh casually.

He eyed me blatantly. "A pretty piece of ass you've got there," he said in Russian. "But you didn't need her. We could have given you something maybe not as good-looking but a hell of a lot younger."

Stosh flushed. "I don't like you speaking about this lady in that fashion. I think you owe her an apology," he said in Russian.

"Kurite moju trubku," he said insolently. "She doesn't understand Russian anyway."

"But I do," said Stosh angrily, turning bright red. Yury had just used a vulgar expression which means "suck my dick."

He smiled, showing three gold teeth, and bowed elaborately. *"Izviniti pazhalsta."* Please excuse me.

Throughout this exchange, I managed to keep my face blank. Believe me, it was tough. I clenched my fists under the table in order to resist the strong desire to deck the bastard. I was the junior girls' boxing champ at Camp High Point for two years running, but the guy was built like a kiosk, so hitting him probably wasn't a great idea. I had not told Stosh that I understood Russian. He was appealing, but he was also Mafia. Mistakenly placed trust could be fatal.

I couldn't tell if the goon recognized me. At the factory I had worn my hair pulled back and had on only lipstick. Now my hair was long and loose and I had applied the whole nine yards of makeup. Men are usually not that observant, but the guy had those Stalin-like Georgian eyes that are merely slits, so that subtle nuances of reaction were impossible to read.

They had the usual man-type brief conversation and then Stosh took me by the arm and I said a smiling good night and we left.

When we got outside, I could feel Stosh's tension. "I'm sorry you had to go through that. The man's an animal."

"Don't be upset. I had myself Scotchgarded years ago against pigs like him." Then I put my arm through his. "I think it's sweet that you're concerned. Who is he anyway?"

"His name is Yury Berezov. He's Nickonov's hatchet man. Or knife man would be more accurate. He loves only two things—knives and birds."

"Birds? Alive or stuffed? Does he use the knives to kill birds?"

"No, only people. He's a master at it. He was an emergency medic during Soviet days and learned the vulnerable spots to insert a knife in order to inflict instant death. As for birds, he loves them. It may be hard to believe, but that ugly brute is an avid bird-watcher."

I could see that the encounter with Berezov had

unnerved him. Was it me he was upset about or the fact that he was seen with me by Nickonov's man? I was a bit shaken myself. The sense of ruthless violence the man emitted was unsettling if not downright scary.

Stosh stopped and put his arms around me. "Let's go home."

When we got to the hotel, he accompanied me to my door and started to say good night. Then he looked at me plaintively. "Could we just have a nightcap?"

He was still wound up and upset, so I invited him in. My room had a cozy setup of a couch, coffee table, and mini-bar.

"That Melodi Club looked like a very lavish and successful operation," I said. "The place was packed and it's not even Saturday night."

"It's like that every night. That and the other one at the Continental Hotel."

"So this wasn't your first visit to these clubs."

He nodded. "We checked them out about a year ago."

"To what end?"

He smiled grimly. "A hostile takeover."

"I gather you decided they were not your cup of tea."

"Not mine anyway. I'm only involved in tech stuff."

I shook my head. "I find it difficult to accept your speaking of your business as though it's a legitimate moral one."

He stiffened and I saw the fire ignite in his eyes.

Here it comes, but at least it'll take his mind off our nightclub visit.

"Taxes are legitimate, aren't they? Businesses pay taxes. Where does that tax money go? To the government. Why? For the purpose of running the government to assure a good stable life for me and my family. Right? But if instead that money is going illegitimately into private pockets, the system has broken down. Then I must handle the matter directly by collecting taxes myself and using them to ensure that same stable comfortable life that my government has failed to provide me."

"That's got to be the most specious reasoning I ever heard."

Then he said very seriously, "No, it's just convoluted self-justification. How else do you think I could live with myself?"

We looked at each other and started to laugh, which became more and more a frantic release of our tensions. Before we knew it, we were undressing each other in a frenzy. He went back to his room about three A.M.

After he left, I was too exhausted to think through what had just happened, but I felt disquieted, which would probably mean a restless sleep. There was no doubt that we were both very attracted to each other, but I don't go in for casual sex. However, there's nothing like danger to heighten passions to the point of overcoming reason. Never fear, no amount of lust dulls my brain to the point of overlooking the need for safe sex.

• • •

WE MET THE next morning at breakfast, which in Finland is a fantastic buffet with an almost overwhelming selection of cheeses, fish, sausages, ham, eggs, cereals, fruits, breads, doughnuts, muffins, and yogurts. It's dastardly. When you read the huge breakfast selection on an American diner menu, it's just words. It's hard to make a choice, but you do. However, when you see it all laid out temptingly before you, it's almost impossible to resist trying a little of everything. I know I sometimes come off as superwoman, but I have my weaknesses—and this is one. I stuffed myself until I could barely move. Was I sorry? Sure. Would I do it again? Of course.

We left from Saarinen's red-and-green granite railroad station and took the Pendolino to Hanko. This is a high-speed electric train that runs on smooth new tracks between Helsinki and Turku and is the height of comfort in train travel. After a two-hour trip, we stepped out into the small village that is the southernmost point in Finland, situated where the Baltic Sea and the Gulf of Finland meet. One of the natives later told me that on days when the water of the sea is too chilly to swim in, they merely walk across town to the gulf, which will be warmer.

We took separate rooms at the Hotel Regatta, which is about one hundred feet from the beach. I stepped out onto my balcony and noticed a small group of people sitting on the rocks at the water's edge looking up at the sky. All of them had binoculars and I recalled that Hanko is a noted spot for bird migration. I always admired the patience of birdwatchers, who are perfectly willing to sit for hours to catch sight of a particular avian species. They were so busy looking up that they apparently didn't see what looked like a large fish swimming in the cold water. Suddenly it emerged, and was a man, who proceeded to remove his bathing suit, dry himself, put on clothes, and walk calmly away. I'm intrigued with the Finns' sangfroid, and you can take that literally and figuratively. Having grown up in a country where nudity is regarded as shameful, I envy their unselfconscious attitude that the body is something totally natural.

Stosh knocked on my door. "Come, let's rent bicycles and ride around town. We have plenty of time. With that massive intake for breakfast, I don't think you'll be ready for lunch for a while."

"As I recall, you made about five hits on the buffet tables yourself," I said.

It was a perfect spring day. The dark blue ocean met the light blue sky as far as you could see. I pointed out the bird-watchers to him.

"Yes, they gather here in the morning and again in the evening when the birds mass."

We rode along the beaches that were studded with individual red-and-green-roofed wooden changing rooms. Europeans do not sit around in wet bathing suits because they believe this causes rheumatism, so they change shortly after each swim. If the beaches were only for locals, I imagine these little rooms wouldn't be necessary, given their attitude toward removing their clothes in public. But Hanko is an international resort and brings visitors from all over the world who may not share the same free attitude.

"Look at those enchanting houses," I said, pointing to the buildings that overlooked the beach. "They look like huge elaborately decorated cakes."

Some were private homes, some were small inns. They were large sprawling pastel-colored wooden structures in pale greens, yellows, pinks. Each displayed intricate architectural details in the form of carved filigree designs in varied shapes and sizes.

"I read somewhere that they're called *pitsihuvila* and were common building design elements at the beginning of the century," I said. "Every rich merchant had to outdo the other with more elaborate designs than his neighbor."

"I thought the Finns shunned ostentation," said Stosh.

"These are just a mild conceit—hardly comparable to the opulent gold, silver, and marble in the homes of Russian aristocrats. It's only wood and it's art, in a sense."

"Actually," said Stosh as we stood and admired one of the houses, a tall four-story building with many wings and cupolas, "Hanko has had a long history with Russia. Did you notice the outcroppings of red stone along the beach? That is Hanko granite, which was quarried and machined here for many monuments in St. Petersburg. The town was also a popular spa that the Russian nobility visited for health cures in the early nineteenth century. As a matter of fact, I've been thinking of buying a house here myself. Some of my associates already have."

There goes the neighborhood. The poor Finns. They have been fighting off takeovers for centuries.

The Russians couldn't do it by force, now it looks like they may do it with money.

The streets were quiet since it was off season, and we cycled in companionable silence, enjoying the smells of the sea and the cries of the birds. Unlike Scarsdale and Greenwich, where one-and two-acre zoning ensures ghettos of affluence, we saw simple bungalows next to elaborate houses. It is part of the lovely nature of the Finns to pay little attention to class distinctions. As we cycled inland a bit we came to the official buildings, which looked quite new, a fact I commented upon.

"They owe these new buildings to us, the Russians," he said laconically. "The library, police headquarters, and city hall . . . we blew up all the old ones after we occupied and then left the town after World War II."

"The Russians came here? Why?"

"The army thought it would be an ideal location for a strategic base. But unfortunately for us, communication systems were not what they are now and the remoteness of the town made all our equipment inoperable and unable to access the rest of our army. There were no satellites in those days, you know. So we pulled out. But not before we left them this memento of our stay." He stopped before a massive blocklike stone structure that resembled a tomb. "This is called the Russian Memorial and is a popular tourist spot for visitors who come to marvel at the sheer grotesque ugliness of it. We blew up everything else."

"Aren't you just a little bit concerned about your

welcome here if you buy a house? Somehow I don't think the neighbors will be rushing in with cups of kasha.''

He shrugged. ''The Finns are an extraordinary people. They are bordered by two countries that have been trying to take them over for centuries, six hundred years under Swedish rule, one hundred years under czarist rule. Their attitude has been to accept both cultures philosophically and take something from each. Swedish is a second language here, and the country is dotted with Eastern Orthodox churches. I'm not worried.''

We resumed our ride and saw very few people along the way. It was delightfully peaceful and had that special quiet of resort towns where you can almost hear the sighs of relief from the natives after the tourists depart and they once more have their village to themselves.

We rode around to the main harbor that was filled with ships and boats of all sizes and shapes, from kayaks to yachts. Stosh explained that Hanko has a very active harbor because it has the longest ice-free period in all of Finland.

''Is this where you pick up your Mercedes?'' I asked.

''BMW,'' he corrected. ''Yes, tomorrow.''

''Do you fellows break bottles of champagne over your fenders?''

''Which fellows?'' he asked.

''All the 'New Russians' and Mafia who will gather here to celebrate. Isn't this some sort of holiday, when you all get together to pick up your fifty-thousand-dollar cars?''

"If Mr. Soros lives up to his newest promise of giving us five hundred million dollars in the next two years, I think we'll all be picking up Rolls-Royces next year," he said with a straight face.

"Why don't you guys just give him the numbers of your Swiss bank accounts and arrange for direct deposit?" I said.

By this time it was four o'clock. "Since we skipped lunch, why don't we have an early dinner?" said Stosh. "We'll go to the Origo. It's a charming fish restaurant right over there on the pier."

"Fine—I'd like a little lie-down and shower," I said. "How about we meet at six?"

"You go back to the hotel—I want to pick up some seashells for my little sister Masha. I'll knock on your door at six."

As I lay on my bed I thought about my companion. He was highly intelligent, attractive, sweet, young, a wonderful and tender lover—and a murderer. Although the killings may not have been committed by his hand, they were involved in his work and possibly ordered by him. It was hard to reconcile the two pictures. What the hell, Ivan the Terrible was probably a doting father and I understand Hitler was wonderful to his mother.

By six, I was ready and waiting. I had dressed casually in a cream-colored fisherman's turtleneck sweater and black corduroy jeans and light makeup. By six-fifteen, he hadn't come and I was a bit annoyed. I'm one of those compulsive on-time types and I expect the same consideration from others. The room was getting stuffy, so I stepped out on the balcony. I looked down the beach. That's funny—that looked like Stosh's bicycle sprawled out on the sand. I dashed out of my room and ran along the beach toward the bike. No sign of Stosh, but a handful of shells were strewn around one of the little changing-room sheds. My stomach tightened and I walked up to it. The door was shut and I opened it slowly. He was slumped on the bench inside. I didn't have to look twice to realize he was dead, but I touched for a pulse—none. There was no blood, no sign of struggle. He looked untroubled, unsurprised, as though he had fallen peacefully asleep. Then I saw the almost imperceptible slit on the left side of his jacket.

I looked quickly around me—not a soul in sight. I quickly picked up his bicycle and rode furiously to the police station as though someone was after me. Perhaps he was.

"There's a murdered man on the beach in one of those little changing rooms," I said more calmly than I felt. The policeman at the front desk was dumbfounded. He looked at me to see if I was either drunk or mad, and then dashed into the office behind him and came out in seconds with a tall, dark-haired, mustached police officer.

"I am *Rikos Tarkastaja Laaksonen,*" he said. The first two words were his title—crime inspector—the last was his name. "My *konstaapeli* here tells me you wish to report a body on the beach." Although he probably never had to deal with anything more than tickets for overtime parking and DWI, he was as cool and equable as if I were reporting a lost kitten. I know Finns are laid-back, but I would have liked just a little mild hysteria to greet my announcement.

"How do you know he's been murdered?" he asked.

"I'll show you when we get there," I answered.

He called out instructions in Finnish to his *konstaapeli* and a policewoman who had come in. I got into a car with them. The SOC (scene-of-the-crime) team would probably follow once he established this was not the ravings of some imaginative tourist who had been reading too many Agatha Christies.

He stopped the car a distance away from the small changing hut so as not to disturb whatever clues I hadn't already inadvertently destroyed. He put on gloves, approached the door, and opened it slowly. When he didn't react for a few minutes, I thought, Ye gods, is this going to be one of those movie scenes where the body has disappeared and everyone is going to look at me like I'm some kind of loony nutcase?

He stepped back and said something to the officers, who were standing patiently by, and they immediately started putting yellow scene-of-the-crime tape around the area.

"What made you think he didn't die of a heart attack?" he asked.

"The slash in his jacket over his heart. That looks like an entry point for a knife."

He nodded. "I noticed that too." Then he looked at me curiously. "You are unusually observant."

I said nothing. There was no question there and one

of my inviolate rules is never to volunteer information.

"You know this man?" he asked me.

I nodded. "He's Russian. Those seashells are his," I said, pointing to the sand. "He was collecting them to take home to his little sister." I felt tears stinging my cheeks. The inspector said something to the policewoman and she came over to me solicitously. I noted she had more stripes on her sleeve than the policeman.

She saw that I noticed. "We may outrank them, but we're always the ones expected to give aid and comfort," she said with a smile.

"They still see us as the gentler sex," I said. "Many times that works to our advantage."

We stood aside for a short time and the inspector approached me.

"What is your name, please, and may I see your passport."

"My name is Emma Rhodes and my passport is upstairs in my room right over there." I pointed to the hotel.

"*Rikos Komisario Vuori* will take you to fetch it. Then you will please come back to the police station with me."

"All right, but first there's something I must do." I walked back to the little hut and picked up the seashells where Stosh had apparently dropped them when he was slain. "I think his little sister would like to have these. I'm sure she would like to know that the last thing he was thinking of was her."

We returned to the station and they sat me in a

121

room with a cup of steaming coffee. *Rikos Vuori* took out a notebook as she, I, and the inspector sat around a table in a pleasant room. I was being treated as a visitor rather than a suspect. Of course, that could change at any moment. I am well aware that the person who finds the body is regarded as the primary suspect.

"You knew the victim very well?"

Implication—were you lovers?

"We met two days ago in St. Petersburg through mutual friends."

Implication—it wasn't some quickie pickup but the result of a respectable introduction.

"What was his name?"

I told him.

"What brought you both to Hanko at this time of year?"

"He came to pick up his car tomorrow. I came along because I wanted to see more of Finland than Helsinki."

He looked at me approvingly. So far I was doing fine.

"Then he was fairly well-off," said the inspector.

I looked at him evenly. "He was Mafia."

There was a small gasp from *Rikos Vuori* and raised eyebrows from her boss. It was nice to see that something could stir them besides Puccini.

He said something to her and she left the room. "You came by train to Hanko?"

"Yes, this morning on the Pendolino."

My God—was it really just this morning? He was fiddling with a paper clip. I could see he was marking time and waiting for something. Or someone. The policewoman returned and nodded to him happily. "He'll be here within fifteen minutes. He's in Karjaa."

The inspector arose, looking relieved. "We will ask you to wait here for a while for the arrival of my superior. May we get you more coffee, perhaps a sandwich?"

Well, they're not getting out the rubber hose yet. I suddenly remembered I hadn't eaten since breakfast, albeit a sumptuous one.

"A sandwich would be fine," I said.

He left and the policewoman sat down to stay with me.

"Oh, I just remembered," I said. "We were going to have dinner at six at the restaurant Origo, and knowing Stosh, he made a reservation. Could you cancel that for us, please?"

Was I well brought up or what? My mother did such a job of instilling manners and consideration (which are actually the same) that if I came down with salmonella poisoning after someone's dinner party, I'd undoubtedly spend my first respite between upchucks writing a thank-you note to my hostess.

The door opened and a tall slender man with graying hair entered the room followed by the inspector. The policewoman jumped to her feet.

"*Hei*, sir," she said.

Pronounced "hey," the word is Finnish for "hello," which makes everyone sound really hip.

He nodded to her and then introduced himself. "I

123

am Detective Chief Superintendent Jarmo Valtonen of the *Keskusrikospolisi*.''

Are you getting the hang of Finnish? Notice the end of the word often tells the story. *Keskus* means "central," *rikos* means "crime," and of course, *polisi* means "police." The *Keskusrikospolisi* is Finland's National Bureau of Investigation. They are customarily called in by local police for cases that require facilities beyond their capability and expertise, or with international overtones, as this one had.

"How did you know the victim was Mafia?" he asked.

Let's skip the small talk—bang, we're off.

"He told me."

"Was he here in Hanko on business?"

"His primary reason, as far as I know, was to pick up his new BMW," I answered. "But isn't his business somewhat like yours, Superintendent, in that you are never 'off duty'?"

"Do you work with him?" he asked.

"No."

"Then why did you come?"

"To see Hanko. It sounded charming."

"You both came from St. Petersburg to Helsinki? Why?"

The *momento de verdad*—the moment of truth. Should I tell him the whole story? I had to review the ramifications quickly. As I weighed the situation I could see no harm in revealing the whole truth. Moreover, I could see less danger to me if I did so. There was no question in my mind about who committed the murder—the bullhead from the Melodi last night.

He would never do anything on his own but was probably working under instructions from Nickonov. My guess was the creep did recognize me after all and reported that to Nickonov. Seeing me at the factory and then together with Stosh was the kind of coincidence that sends off warning signals to Mafia groups whose survival depends on vigilance and virtual paranoia. It indicated signs of collusion between Stosh's *gruoppirovka* and the Tsvetnuye, which Nickonov must have concluded portended an intended takeover and thus sealed Stosh's death warrant since the deal would never fly without him. Since I was obviously involved in the secret operation, I should also have been on their hit list. The stiletto method of killing matched that of Irina, which could mean Abba was right and the knife was meant for me.

The horrible thought struck me that I had been responsible for two deaths—Irina in place of me, and Stosh for being with me. Maybe I should have remained a lawyer. The only life-threatening aspect of that job was the possibility of dying from exhaustion from that twelve-hour-a-day-seven-days-a-week work schedule.

"Superintendent, let me save you the trouble of figuring out what to ask me. Allow me to tell you everything."

When I got through with my saga, he had one question. "You are a private what?"

I sighed. Here we go again. "Private Resolver." I explained my profession. The only thing I held back was the identity of my client, of course. He asked, but was not surprised or persistent when I refused.

The door opened and a *konstaapeli* handed him a paper. He read it for a moment and then looked at me. My pedigree, no doubt. Thanks to the U.S. Freedom of Information Act, Interpol, and the Internet, every detail of anyone's life is available for the asking. I wonder if the report included that I bit Jeffrey Block in fourth grade when he tried to play doctor with me. On the arm, of course.

"You seem to have led a rather unusual life, Miss Rhodes. I can't figure out if you're like one of those harmless fictional detectives like that TV lady Jessica Fletcher who happens upon violence, or a dangerous individual who causes it."

"You'll find I'm neither, Superintendent. I am a professional who works for money and not thrills."

He eyed me speculatively. "I would like to believe you. However, nothing in your background material assures me that you are not involved in this murder or, in fact, that you did not commit it."

Time to bring in the big guns. "Would it help if you checked me out with Detective Chief Superintendent Caleb Franklin of Scotland Yard?" I asked.

His eyes widened. "You know him?"

"Quite well." You'll never know how well, I thought. "Why don't you phone him now? I believe he'll vouch for my reliability and authenticity. Here's his private number," and I reached into my bag and took out my Filofax.

To say he was impressed was understatement. After all, there aren't too many people who carry around the private phone number of one of the hottest names in law enforcement.

Caleb Franklin is one of the stars of Scotland Yard. His progress within that hallowed institution is all the more remarkable because he is a public-schooled Cambridge black man who earned his way to the top of an organization that resents elitists and minorities. Like the fictional Inspector Morse, he is highly regarded for his brilliant record of solved homicides. Unlike Morse, he is amiable, charming, and beset by adoring women.

The Finnish detective chief superintendent spoke to the British detective chief superintendent for a few minutes. Then he handed me the phone with a big smile. That looks hopeful.

"Superintendent Franklin wishes to speak with you."

"Awash with dead bodies again, Emma? Corpses seem to cling to you like limpets."

"What's so surprising?" I asked. "It's my business. If I was a dentist, it would be teeth."

He laughed. "A charming picture. Who is the deceased?"

"A highly regarded and skilled member of the Russian Mafia."

I could almost hear him sitting up in his chair. "Good Lord. I thought you were in Finland."

"A hop, skip, and a jump from St. Petersburg. We flew here yesterday."

"From that am I to draw that your case is in Russia?"

"Right."

"Then I suggest you withdraw from the case immediately. Emma, my love, you are in the Wild Wild

West. You've stepped up to a shoot-out at the O.K. Corral without a weapon. There is no law in Russia today; the Mafia functions unchecked. If you displease them, they immediately correct the error of your ways by a highly effective method: they kill you.''

"So I've learned."

"What's your connection to the victim?"

"Recent and tenuous."

"Do the people who killed him know that?"

"I'm afraid not."

"Please, let me talk to Superintendent Valtonen," he said in a terse voice.

Valtonen listened intently and looked over at me with concern. He nodded. "Yes, I agree. Thank you, Superintendent." He handed me the phone again.

"I told him you will need close guarding until they catch the killer. Much as I'd love to suggest you come here to London, I'm afraid you'll still be too accessible to them. Emma, please take the next plane home to the U.S. Infrequent as our meetings may be, they're stellar and I should hate to lose you. In the interim, I am perfectly happy to function as your personal reference bureau.''

Caleb and I have a lovely time together whenever I'm in residence in my London flat. We met during a case of mine in Brussels* and West Wycombe, and have been close, and I mean close, friends ever since.

The *konstaapeli* came in and handed a paper to the superintendent. He read it quickly and said to me,

*Noblesse Oblige

"You were correct. This is the autopsy report. The victim died from a sharp stilettolike wound straight into the heart."

"Was there a bruise on his head?" I asked.

"Yes. How did you know?"

"The assailant would have had to sneak up on his prey—easy on the quiet sand when the victim would have been concentrating on looking down for shells. Stosh was too wary to allow anyone to get close enough to stab him. He had to have been knocked unconscious first. There were no dragging marks in the sand, so the killer probably hefted the body over his shoulder and deposited him in the changing hut. I imagine he hid him there to delay discovery in order to gain enough time to get away from Hanko."

He looked at me admiringly. "Very succinctly put, Ms. Rhodes. You are obviously a professional."

I expressed surprise at the speed with which they came up with postmortem results.

He smiled. "I would like to credit that to American-like efficiency, but I'm afraid the rapid report is due to the fact that I happen to have been on a case in the nearby town. Since it is a very small village, they have absolutely no investigative facilities, so I brought my *oileuslaakari* with me—that's our word for medical examiner."

He turned to the policewoman. "*Rikos Komisario,* please go to her hotel with Miss Rhodes while she packs her things and then put her in my car. I will be taking her back to Helsinki with me."

"What will you do about Mr. Chirkasov?" I asked.

I hated to refer to Stosh as a body; it's so dehumanizing.

"He will be subjected to a more thorough autopsy and then the body will be released to the family."

"Then how will the case proceed?" Now that I'd established my quasi-professional standing, plus a relationship with a highly regarded law-enforcement officer, I was certain he would not regard my question as presumptuous or inappropriate. I was right; he gave me the full answer.

"We will contact the Russian RUOP, which is their commissariat unit handling professional criminals. Of course, the Russian embassy in Helsinki will be notified. They have a resident Russian policeman on their premises. No other embassy has such a staff member, but we have been getting so much Russian crime here that we all deemed it necessary."

"I assume you will leave an investigative team here to find out if anyone saw anything," I said.

"Of course. They have already started knocking on doors in the surrounding houses to ask if anyone suspicious was seen in the vicinity."

"Maybe I can give your people a head start by suggesting they ask about a specific man," I said.

"Who is this man?" the superintendent asked.

"He is a Mafia killer who is skilled with the knife and could have been ordered to assassinate the victim. He's the man I told you about whom we met last night at the Melodi Club." I described him to the *rikos komisario*, who took careful notes.

The superintendent started issuing orders to his staff and then explained his instructions to me. "I put a man on the train that will leave shortly for Helsinki, but I imagine our suspect came and has left by car. Since we don't know what make of car he has, road-blocks are useless. We will have someone at the Melodi nightclub and at Helsinki-Vantaa Airport in case he attempts to fly back to St. Petersburg.''

''Perhaps you should check the three gas stations in Hanko to see if someone matching his description stopped there. He'll undoubtedly need to fill up for the trip back, and then you'll find out what kind of car he drives.''

He looked at me for a second and barked out instructions to the *rikos komisario*. As we got into his car he said to his driver ''Helsinki-Vantaa Airport.'' I assumed that was to be my destination. During the two-hour ride he told me the detailed police procedures that would take place once they caught the suspect.

In Finland, a murder suspect can be held legally for three days. After that, if the police need more time to gather evidence, a judge may grant them two more weeks of suspect incarceration while they gather sufficient evidence to present the case to a *syyttaja* (prosecutor). The prosecutor can file one of two charges: *murha*, which is murder and must be proven to premeditated, or *tappo*, which is manslaughter. They do not have capital punishment, which did not surprise me. But what did was the fact that they have no life imprisonment. A guilty murderer is sentenced to a maximum of sixteen years. When I asked how many murders they had last year, he told me a total of 170 in the entire country. The figure sounded a little unrealistically rosy, but I've always rated statistics among the creative sciences. He also claimed that Russia had thirty thousand contract killings last year. Now, that's a figure I could believe.

As we were approaching the outskirts of Helsinki the call came in that the Russian had been apprehended. A man of his description driving a Mercedes had stopped for gas at the station at the edge of Hanko and he was picked up by the police at Pasila, close to Helsinki.

The superintendent was jubilant. He turned to me and asked if I would come to the central police station to make a positive identification from a lineup. It took all of fifteen seconds. I took one look at the group of burly brutes they had assembled for the occasion and picked out our boy. Superintendent Valtonen could not conceal his satisfaction. They took me into a room and taped my statement, shook my hand, and sent me off in an official car.

The superintendent thanked me and assured me that I would not be needed to testify at the trial. If there will be one, I thought. Actually, what could I contribute other than the fact that I saw the alleged perpetrator the night before at the Melodi Club? That he and Stosh belonged to rival Mafia *gruoppirovkas* would only be hearsay and would be for the Finnish police to prove. For that they would need the help and cooperation of the Russian police, which is an oxymoron. Good luck to them. I had little faith in their potential ability to lock up the bastard.

When the police driver drove me to the airport, he dropped me off at the section where flights go to the

U.S. I thanked him and headed for the ticket desk, where I purchased a one-way to St. Petersburg.

Maybe you think I'm off my rocker to go back to Russia. Don't think I don't half agree with you. I spent part of the drive to the airport evaluating my choices. Sure my life would be in danger there. By now, Nickonov and his *gruoppirovka* knew their man had been arrested and undoubtedly figured I partici- pated in the fingering. If they had Stosh killed for being seen with me, then they knew I had some in- volvement with the Tsvetnuye Metalluy. Perhaps they would suspect that I was in St. Petersburg to pry into their operation, else why would I be out there at the factory and the Melodi Club? They may not know why, I thought, I could be some nosy journalist, but in any case, I constituted a threat to their juicy little plum arrangement. And we all know how the Mafia handles threats.

So Caleb was right in telling me to get the hell out of Russia.

But here's the critical kernel of my decision- making dilemma. I've been in tight situations before, where my life was threatened, and accepted them as going with the territory. But this time I wasn't deal- ing with some semiamateur terrorists who are big on causes but low on killing skills. Nor was I in a country where an effective police force acted as a deterrent. I was facing the deadly Russian Mafia, ruth- less trained killers operating in a country where no restraints inhibited their murderous activities. Posing a risk to a criminal group in a lawless society is like flying on a trapeze without a net. It ain't healthy.

The real question is, is a Private Resolver a total professional or just some la-di-da dilettante sleuth who takes off at the first sign of danger? If I didn't stick it out to find out who was really behind all this, then I should just take down my shingle. And another thing—how do you and I know that my analysis as outlined above is accurate? So far, it's all conjecture and what is known as educated guesses. Actually, I have no proof to back my assumptions. Maybe Irina's murder was not a case of mistaken identity and she and not I was the intended victim. Maybe Stosh was murdered because of an internecine battle between *gruoppirovkas* that had nothing to do with the Tsvetnuye and me. And maybe I'm becoming some hare-brained paranoic who sees an assassin behind every bush.

That does it. The decision is made. Yes, I admit to being scared shitless. Wouldn't you? But I am going back to St. Petersburg. There, aren't you proud of me? I am.

VII

―❦―

"EMMA, YOU'RE BACK!"

Aleksei was coming down the stairs just as I walked in the door. He hugged me and placed a kiss on each cheek.

"How was your trip?"

"Interesting," I answered.

"You're just in time. Abba and I are about to have *chai*."

"You're still here?" I asked in surprise as we walked into the salon where tea had been set up.

Abba was sprawled out comfortably on a couch. "The accommodations were so good and the company so pleasant, I decided to stay on a little longer," he said. "Besides, the princess has decided to have the Easter ball Sunday after all, and I didn't want to miss that."

Cynthia Smith

All the time he was speaking so lightly, I saw his sharp eyes looking at me intently.

"Irina's parents insisted that we go ahead," said Aleksei. "Actually, cancellation would have been a nightmare. Mother's celebration is a tradition and royalty will be coming from all over Europe. It would be difficult to reach everybody in time."

I didn't feel like sitting down to have tea and small talk; there was too much for me to think over. But I did feel like having tea and *mazovezky prianiki,* which are delicious little rye honey cakes. I ate my fill, and rose to leave, pleading weariness. I had contributed almost nothing to the conversation, but fortunately Abba could keep up enough chatter to entertain a conclave of monks who have taken a vow of silence.

Abba arose, too. "I'll walk you upstairs. I have a few messages to give you."

I figured. To Abba, my silence was undoubtedly more eloquent than if I had screamed and tore at my hair. The moment we got out of Aleksei's earshot, he began.

"O.K., *ahuvati*. What happened? From the look of you, it's big-time *tsuras*."

He came into my room and sat down, and I told him. His face took on that intent look that meant his computer brain was absorbing and evaluating all the data being fed into it. When I finished, he looked thoughtful and was silent for a minute.

"Then they didn't want to kill you. If that was on the schedule, he would have knocked off Stosh on the beach and then followed you up to your room and finished the job."

I nodded. "Yes, I thought of that. I must say I'm relieved. It's pleasant but puzzling."

"Don't start doing the *kazotzky* yet, *sharmuta*. You're not out of the woods by a long shot. Notice I said they didn't want to kill you—I didn't say they don't. The timing may not yet be right, but the intent is still there."

"You mean my future is not yet secure?"

"Sure, as secure as a Hasid at a skinhead rally. They must now know you're involved with that colored-metal plant and are probably aware that you're out here to suss their miserable operation. What they don't know is how you intend to use your knowledge. Do you intend to advise their benefactor to stop benefacting? Or did you plan to transfer your support to Stanislaus's *gruoppirovka*?"

Then it hit me. "Of course. If I was working to tie in with Stosh, that would mean I'm flexible. Translation—crooked."

"Which would mean," finished Abba, "that you're a buyable commodity and they'll be waiting for the proper moment to broach the subject of how much you want to join their partnership."

"But wouldn't it be easier, let alone cheaper, to get rid of me?"

"You could be far more valuable to them alive. Think of how you would solidify their position with Brannock if you went home and told him everything was hotsy-totsy here. You could be their insurance policy to keep things rolling indefinitely."

"Wow, Abba, I'd be an instant millionaire," I said

with a big smile. "What color Mercedes will you want?"

"You'd be more than a millionaire," said Abba. "Like the Hebrew teacher who was asked what he'd do if he got Rothschild's money. 'If I had Rothschild's money, I'd be even richer than Rothschild because I wouldn't give up my teaching.' You wouldn't have to give up the thirty thou from Brannock."

I sat down on my bed. "Then I can expect someone from the Lomonosov Mafia to approach me shortly."

"Not just someone. The boss—the big honcho."

"You mean Nickonov?"

"No," said Abba. "I know Vladimir well. He's cunning, he's shrewd, but he doesn't have the savvy to run a major operation like this. It's big business, sweetheart, and it needs a more skilled and sophisticated brain than he has."

"So I'm safe until then."

"Who the fuck knows?" he said. "This is all our conjecture. With these wild Russians, who the hell can tell what goes on in their shitheads? Just don't relax your guard."

"Great. That gives me time to take care of two important things."

"What?"

"Who killed Irina and why. And what to wear to the ball tomorrow night."

"Well, it's good to see you have your priorities right. But why are you mixing in Irina's death?"

"If the little scenario you and I just worked out is accurate, then her murder could have had nothing to do with me. Or maybe it still fits and they were trying to give me a scare and a warning. I understand these Mafia people are ruthless enough to kill innocents to make examples. Maybe they offed Stosh while he was with me for the same reason, so that by the time they approached me I'd be a trembling pushover for whatever deal they offered."

"So you want to find out if some persons unknown committed the foul deed," said Abba.

I sighed. "It's highly unlikely, isn't it, considering the fact that both murders were committed with the same weapon."

"No, the stiletto is a favorite weapon around these parts and it doesn't necessarily mean the same perpetrator."

"Aleksei gave me the names of Irina's friends and lover. I'll ask him where to find them and then I'm off tomorrow morning at the crack of dawn. Right now I think I'll hit the sack."

I MET GALINA Kodorofsky and Genek Sobchak in a small café on the Bolshoy Prospekt near the university. They were students and could only meet me between classes. The place looked like student hangouts the world over—dark, smoky; and filled with intense conversations and loud music. They had described themselves to me, but knowing the similarity of students, work shirts and jeans, I told them to look for me.

"Miss Rhodes?" A six-foot, four-inch beanpole of a young man with a close-cropped Russian-style haircut stood in front of me.

"Genek Sobchak?"

He smiled. "You were right. There are many of us but only one of you," and he looked at me admiringly. I had nixed the jeans routine in favor of a Karl Lagerfeld navy wool pantsuit. Different, but not ostentatiously chic. "Come, we are over there in the corner."

"This is Galina," he said, introducing me to a young woman in her late twenties with long red hair, green eyes, and pale freckled skin. She held out her hand and smiled and I noticed she was a beauty.

"You are both graduate students?" I asked. They looked too old to be undergraduates.

"Yes."

"In what is your degree?" I asked. "What are you studying?"

"Computer science," they answered simultaneously.

"Do you know Professor Anatoly Yakolov?" I asked.

Something flicked across both their faces. "Yes, of course," they said. "Everyone knows him, he's the chairman of the department."

Interesting reaction.

"It was terrible about Irina," said Galina. "I understand you were with her at the Kirov when it happened."

"Yes, that's why I want to find out why she was killed."

"We wondered why you wanted to talk to us. Why should it concern you?"

I had worked out my game plan beforehand, of

course. When you're planning to interview someone, you damned well better think through your opening gambit to convince them of the righteousness of your cause or they'll never open up. Improvisation comes later. Once they've gotten over their initial skepticism, their reticence usually disappears and then you can fly by the seat of your pants.

"Because I think she may have been killed instead of me."

Their eyes widened. "You mean a mistaken identity?" asked Genek.

"But you do not look alike at all," said Galina.

"Maybe not," I said, "if the assailant knew us both."

"Yes, of course," said Genek thoughtfully. "By description alone, you could pass for each other. Both tall, brown hair, brown eyes, and beautiful."

"And accompanied by Prince Aleksei," added Galina.

"So you see, if she died in my place, not only is that a horrible tragedy for Irina, for which I am dreadfully sorry, but it means I'm still in danger. I want to know that. Of course, it's also possible that she was the intended victim, in which case I'm still sorry, but no longer scared."

They nodded. "We understand. What do you want to know?"

"Was Irina an active member of the communist party?" I spoke softly, but they both looked around quickly. A knee-jerk carryover from the old days, or a realistic current worry? Is Big Brother still listen-

141

ing? Their reaction made it apparent that they, too, were members of the party.

"Yes," said Genek.

"How active?"

"She was the head of our cell and on the board of the central committee in Moscow."

"That's pretty damned active."

They nodded.

"Was she involved in anything special recently that would put her at risk? Something that might cause difficulty for other people or groups?"

They looked at each other. Then, as if by agreement, Genek said, "She was violently against the auctions being held by Yeltsin's government to privatize and sell off some big industries. She had learned the banks had leaked information to some favored millionaires. The whole procedure would be a farce and a betrayal of the people."

"That would earn her some high-powered enemies," I said. "What kind of industries are to be auctioned?"

"Telecommunications and metals."

"How did she make her opposition known?" I asked.

They laughed. "You met Irina and you ask that question?" asked Galina. "She was strong in her beliefs and very forceful in her statements—no matter where. At our cell meetings, she fairly commandeered the floor until you had to agree with her. I never attended a central-committee meeting, but knowing Irina, she would have acted much the same way there.

If Irina had an opinion, it had to be the right one and everyone else had to agree.''

"So we have given you many people who would have liked to see the end of Irina,'' said Genek.

"Specifically who?''

"The yuppies, the New Russians who are our millionaires, the Mafia. Take your pick.''

"How about another direction?'' I asked. ''Like unrequited lovers and broken hearts.''

They looked astonished. ''You can't mean Shura?'' asked Galina.

I nodded. ''She dumped him, didn't she? That had to cause some bitterness.''

Genek got up. ''You must meet Shura. He's right over there.''

Within a few minutes he returned with a man wearing black trousers and shirt, thick silver-rimmed glasses, and carrying a load of books that seemed to bend him over.

"Miss Rhodes, may I introduce you to our friend Shura Petrovnik?''

He extended a wet, limp hand. If I hadn't been wearing my expensive pantsuit, I'd have wiped my hand on the trousers.

"How do you do?''

He sat down carefully. As a child, he must have been been picked on by all the kids on the block. You'd recognize the type—the guy was a born wimp.

"Miss Rhodes was at the Kirov with Irina when she died,'' said Galina gently.

His eyes filled with tears and he sat up and looked at me with interest. ''How was she?'' he asked softly.

The man was in pain, I could see it. "She was happy, vivacious. We had just enjoyed a marvelous first act and she was filled with joy."

He smiled. "I'm glad. I was worried that she ended in anguish."

"No, I was right next to her. The whole awful thing took a second and I assure you she was unaware of what happened to her and had no pain whatsoever."

"Thank you," he said simply.

Well, here's one candidate I can scratch from the roster of suspects. Unless the guy's a better actor than Laurence Olivier, he adored Irina. Besides, the killer was apparently highly skilled and experienced. It took but a single unerring thrust, which meant he knew exactly where to insert the knife. I think this dweeb would have difficulty finding his way out of a paper bag. What on earth did such a gorgeous vibrant woman like Irina see in him?

One last shot. I've been fooled once or twice by people who looked harmless and turned out to be lethal when prodded the wrong way.

"I understand from Prince Aleksei that you were quite upset when Irina broke up with you," I said.

Dr. Jekyll, meet Mr. Hyde. The change in him was startling.

"Prince Aleksei?" His face filled with fury. "Don't even mention his name in the same sentence as Irina's. He's a devil. Her death is all his fault."

"How so?"

"Everything she did was to get his attention. She joined the party because she knew it would get a rise out of him. She fought to get ahead in the party so that he would see how intelligent and capable she really was."

"Are you saying she hated him or was trying to compete with him?"

He spit out the words furiously. "She *loved* him. Passionately, hopelessly."

Galina looked at me sympathetically. "You didn't know, of course. They were sexual partners from childhood. Aleksei deflowered her when she was twelve and he was eighteen. Such a stupid word—how could the casual removal of a blossom from its stem be the description for such a traumatic searing experience?"

"How long did this go on?" I asked.

"Until the day she died."

"Don't you see?" said Shura. "Our relationship, any relationship was impossible. Irina could not feel anything for anyone but him. No other love was real to her, no other man could mean anything to her. She adored him. She worshiped him. Oh, she had her affairs; I was not the first one. As did he. But the difference was his love affairs were whole and normal while hers were merely stopgaps until he was finished with his. The only times he had sex with her or showed any interest in her was between affairs—and that's what she spent her life waiting for."

I remembered how Aleksei sat in the kitchen the night Irina died, crying and seemingly in deep despair. Did he suddenly realize he had truly loved her, as he said, and was suffering the sorrow of one who realizes too late what he had lost? Or were his tears

145

the sadness of a man who was merely bemoaning the closure of a convenience? In either case, the man was a total shit and I'd never be able to look at him the same way again.

VIII

LUNCH WAS A casual buffet because all the servants were busy with frantic preparations for that evening's Easter ball. I found Abba alone at the dining-room table.

"Gosh, it really upsets me to see you off your feed like this," I said as I observed his plate piled with caviar, sausages, *pelmeny,* blini, and kasha.

"Don't criticize. This is a voyage in nostalgia. The food reminds me of my childhood," he said as he tore off a piece of pumpernickel.

"*Shtuyot,*" I said. "Isn't that the Hebrew word for 'bullshit'? Your family could barely afford herring, let alone caviar and sausages aren't kosher."

He looked at the plate of salad I brought over to the table. "Shiksa gourmet fare. How will you manage without Miracle Whip?"

"I am eating lightly. There's bound to be a midnight supper, which could mean four meals today. Unlike your gloriously capacious digestive system, mine closes down after three."

"How did your meeting go this morning?" he asked, wiping sour cream from his beard.

Just then Aleksei walked in. He came over with a smile to kiss my cheek. I must have stiffened, but then I smiled back.

I glanced over at Abba and saw that he had spotted my reaction. It probably only took seconds, but those keen eyes of Abba's missed nothing. That highly honed power of observation undoubtedly saved his life many times.

"Aleksei, have they found any suspects in Irina's murder?" I asked.

He shook his head. "Naturally not. They questioned almost one hundred people who were in the lobby with us. Of course, no one saw anything."

" 'Of course' because there was nothing to see or 'of course' because they wouldn't report anything if they had seen it?" I asked.

"Both. This was undoubtedly a professional killer—probably Mafia. He was too skilled to allow himself to be observed."

"Under those conditions—crowds milling around, groups of people engaged in private conversations—it wouldn't take much skill," said Abba. "King Kong in a suit would've passed unnoticed."

"Not only that," said Aleksei, "but our people have learned to look the other way. Becoming involved is to be avoided at all costs; it can be dangerous in this country. The killer could have just stabbed her and then gone back inside to take his seat for the rest of the ballet. They will never find out who killed her."

"Who knew that you and Irina were going to the Kirov?" I asked.

"Everyone," he said in surprise. "We didn't make it a secret."

"Aleksei, you didn't publish it in the newspapers; the people who knew were only people you and Irina knew."

He hesitated as he figured that out. "Yes, I guess you're right," he said slowly.

"That means either someone or both of you knew, or someone who was specifically told—by someone you both knew."

"Are you saying that one of our friends was responsible for Irina's death?" he asked, aghast.

"Either directly or indirectly."

He shrugged. "What good is all this? Even if I should remember exactly who I told we were going to the ballet, we don't know who Irina told."

"Criminal work consists of narrowing down the field of possible suspects," I said. "It could be painstaking work, but you have to start somewhere. It might help if you could think carefully and come up with the names of everyone you told that you and Irina would be at the Kirov that night."

"All right, if you think it might help," he said. "But later—I cannot do it now. The ball begins tonight at eight," said Aleksei. "I just came in for some coffee. I must get out to the airport to pick up some of the guests. They'll be arriving from everywhere all day.'' He left the room quickly.

''O.K., *tsotskele*—what's with the deep-freeze treatment?'' asked Abba. ''You were talking to him like an Israeli talks to an Arab—out of expediency not friendship. I get the feeling that if you didn't have to deal with him, you'd just as soon see his ass in Siberia. What happened? Did the putz make an uninvited assault upon your maidenhood last night?''

''Not on mine.''

I told him about Irina. His face darkened dangerously. ''Poor kid—doomed at twelve. That *kus-amack* motherfucker. Stalin, where are you when we need you?''

''Abba, I have to see your friend the professor. How do I do that?''

He didn't question but gave me Anatoly's phone number. He lived on Vasilievsky Island, which is a residential area about twenty minutes from downtown. We arranged to meet within an hour in the lobby of the Pribaltiyskaya Hotel, located not too far from his apartment. I kept asking my taxi driver if he knew where he was going, because the area didn't look promising; in fact, it looked downright decrepit and seemed an unlikely site for one of the biggest hotels in St. Petersburg. We drove through rows of starkly ugly blocks of obviously Soviet-built highrises. The few buildings that had the luxury element of balconies displayed not flowers but laundry. There were few people in the streets and no shops or restaurants to be seen. I understood the hotel was once considered the best in the country. How could it be located in this seedy area? Suddenly a massive structure appeared out of the fog that had rolled in off the Gulf of Finland and the cab drew up in front of a sixteen-story monolith fronted by a huge stone staircase that looked like a setting for a Russian movie. I could just see Cossacks riding up the steps to attack. The cab stopped at the foot of the steps.

"Why don't we drive up to the front door of the hotel?" I asked. I didn't fancy walking up that tremendous flight of stairs that were undoubtedly dangerously slippery from the slight drizzle that had just begun.

He shook his head. *"Ya astanaviti z'd'ed."* I stop here. He looked obdurate.

"Why?" I asked.

"Mafia." He explained that the taxi concession in the hotel was run by a Mafia group and only their cabs were permitted to use the special driveway that leads directly to the front doors of the hotel.

"Doesn't the hotel object to their guests being subjected to this inconvenience?"

He shrugged. "Who is the hotel?" he answered. "Mafia."

Incredible. It's like one of those Hollywood movies where a terrorist group takes over a train, building, or major institution and holds it for ransom and the entire country is horrified. Except here the event would raise nary a ripple, because it's not news—it's an everyday occurrence. If you are accustomed to controlled law and order, it's hard to envision living without that security and being forced to accept whatever hardships are imposed upon you by criminal elements.

The Pribaltiyskaya has twelve hundred rooms, which could mean a possible occupancy of 2,400 guests—who all seemed to be in the lobby when I walked in. I assumed they were headed for the fleet of tour buses that waited in front. If you're looking for a quiet, intimate, elegant hotel, this ain't it. The place was a zoo. I walked up to the reception desk for directions to the one of the hotel's six restaurants where I had arranged to meet Anatoly. There were dozens of people standing about hurling questions in many languages at the harried clerks. I tried to await my turn, but I soon realized that there was no such thing as an orderly line—you just pushed in front and yelled. Well, I can holler as loud as the next one, and I had the advantage of yelling in Russian, which got immediate response.

"Gd'e Daugava Restaurant, pazhalsta?"

One of the clerks pointed to a staircase to my right and I moved toward it. As I walked through the lobby I stopped at a large bulletin board, which was filled with notices. I have always been inexorably drawn to posted reading matter. Hang words on a wall and I cannot pass them by. In every hotel room I'm in, I always know the location of the exits and what to do in case of fire (don't touch the doorknobs, whatever you do.) I know the Heimlich maneuver. And I'm always aware of the maximum occupancy of every elevator. The bulletin board carried the daily itineraries of all the resident tours. Just reading their activity-packed schedules was enough to wear me out.

My favorite was the Star Vacation Group, which instructed members to have luggage in front of their doors at four A.M. the next morning, breakfast at five, and on the bus at six in order to catch the seven A.M. train to Helsinki. That's a vacation? The folks were probably out until midnight the night before, because the purpose of any tour is to pack in as many activities as possible. This reads well in the brochure but in actuality results in total exhaustion and an inability to absorb what you see. My grandmother took a tour through Europe many years ago that was designed for first-time travelers who wanted to cover the entire continent in twenty days. I remember her being very upset because she had to go to the bathroom on the bus and missed the entire Black Forest.

The hotel was a mystifying maze of corridors, escalators, and staircases until I finally found the Daugava Restaurant and spotted Anatoly at a table in the corner. He rose and smiled. He was wearing the same outfit, which looked a few days older. Laundry soap is expensive in Russia.

"I ordered coffee, I hope that's all right."

I handed him the bag of seashells. "This is for Masha Chirkasov. A last gift from her brother."

He took it from me and I saw his eyes fill with tears. "Stanislaus was a wonderful young man with a bright future. Such a waste. He was a highly talented engineer who could have accomplished so much for our country."

"If your country would let him. You seem to be systematically destroying your young men."

"Unfortunately, yes."

"They cannot find work here, so they're forced to go into the Mafia. How long had Stosh worked for them?"

"Two years."

"The usual Mafia life span, right?"

He nodded.

"Didn't Stosh know he was making a Faustian deal when he signed on?"

"Probably. But all young men think they're too smart to have it happen to them. They feel they can outwit the devil. They learn too late that no one can."

"Did he have parents?"

"Yes. He will be given a marvelous funeral. The Mafia pride themselves on giving their murdered members a fantastic and expensive send-off."

"Terrific. That and a handful of seashells doesn't sound like much compensation for a son and brother."

He nodded again. "No, it is indeed a sad affair. I really cared for the boy and he was a great help to me professionally, as you know."

"Do you think perhaps that was one of the contributing factors to his murder? Was he giving you information some people didn't want divulged?"

Anatoly shook his head. "No, he was not my only source. All the *gruoppirovkas* fed me facts. As I told you, it was to their advantage. I was their data bank."

"You are almost an icon to your students, aren't you? I get the feeling they worship you."

All right, I was laying it on with a trowel, but I sensed this man thrived on flattery. Like many academicians who find they have a certain charisma for the young, he had developed a conceit that was possibly realistic on campus but somewhat pathetic off it.

"There are always those students who see fit to accept and admire my teachings," he said without a trace of humility.

"Professor, how long had you been the mentor and guru for the Countess Irina Romanov?"

I had caught him totally unawares. My favorite tactic.

"She was not a matriculated student of mine, you know, but she chose to take some of my courses." Only the spilling of some coffee into his saucer betrayed his agitation. "She was a friend of Galina Kodorofsky and Genek Sobchak. They were a sort of inseparable trio. She was quite bright and was very interested in my economic theory of government. I am also professor of economics as well as computer science, you know."

"And what is your theory, Professor?"

He sat up and I could see his eyes light up. Another potential novitiate. Boy, does he have the wrong number. I'm invulnerable when it comes to cults and movements, because I believe too much in my own mind to subordinate it to someone else's.

"I call it 'commucapitalism,' " he said, looking at me like a child awaiting commendation for his cleverness. Gag me with a spoon—I couldn't believe I was hearing such dated twaddle. It was the kind of name my parents could have made up in high school and thought they were Tom Lehrer. I've always felt that members of academia seem to get frozen into an adolescent time warp.

"It consists of recalling many of the structured communist controls over business and labor while allowing a certain proportion of private industry to function," he said.

"What kinds of industries would you privatize, to use the current popular Russian word?"

"Businesses that have technological and economic value to the country."

"You mean like computer companies?"

"Of course, that would be one group."

I remembered something Stosh had told me. "Professor, you have a software development company, don't you?"

He colored. "Yes, but it's just a small affair. We all need some sort of sideline to supplement our salaries or we could not live, you know."

Uh-huh. "And this new government structure, does it also call for certain controls over personal freedom and activities?"

"Only if these activities conflict with the goals of the state."

"And who would determine when they impinge upon each other?"

"The government, of course."

"And who would ensure the proper application of your theory?"

"A well-organized and properly run police and justice system."

"Run by whom?"

"The government, of course."

Sound familiar?

"No checks and balances?"

"Not necessary," he said emphatically.

No, of course not.

"Don't you think my system would be better than what we have now?" he asked.

"Listen, Professor, the Dewey Decimal System would be better than what you have now. But I'm not sure that yours offers much improvement. I grant that you'll abolish certain current failures and wrongs, but you'll only substitute new ones."

"But don't you see?" he said. "We would be able to harness our vast natural resources for the economic and technological benefit of the people instead of allowing them to be exploited and stolen by foreigners and a handful of corrupt individuals who are allowing our heritage to deteriorate."

"What do you mean?"

"Haven't you noticed all those beautiful ancient buildings you see near the Nevsky Prospekt that are cosmetically new on the outside but crumbling inside? They're lived in by the new Russian millionaires who are stealing privatized companies for a song from Yeltsin's corrupt government. Or the Mafia. Neither group cares to restore the entire buildings and thus preserve our national landmarks and heritage. Instead they merely rehabilitate one or two apartments for themselves, often spending millions in order that they alone dwell in decadent luxury. Do they bother to fix up the public rooms of the building, such as the lobbies or courtyards? No. Do they redo the infrastructure of the building? No. But if they don't, won't the pipes burst from time to time and create damage that is very costly to repair? Yes, but why should they care? They'll just patch up the pipes in their own apartments. They live only for themselves and the people be damned.''

His caring and emotion began to make me think perhaps I was misjudging the man's sincerity. Then he went on—and lost me.

"Under my system, we would recover control of our stockpiles of nuclear material."

"To what end?" I asked.

"For the benefit of the People, of course."

"One would have to know the location of the stockpiles. Do you?"

"Of course," he said smugly.

Uh-oh, now he's getting scary.

People with a big *P* meaning everyone, or people with a small *p* meaning a couple of greedy power-hungry guys. Like you, Professor. He is either one of those blue-sky wackos or a dangerous megalomaniac.

"Did Irina support your theory?"

"Of course."

"Did you see her often?"

"She was quite fascinated with my work, you see, and would come over to my home after class to discuss her opinions of my opinions," he said with an engaging smile.

"Didn't your wife object? Irina was a very beautiful woman and not the kind you'd want your husband to be seeing too often."

"My wife died two years ago," he said. "She had been ill for a long time."

"I'm sorry," I said sympathetically. I got the picture. The grieving middle-aged widower and the adoring young aristocratic beauty. A setup straight out of Chekhov.

"Contrary to the conclusion I see in your eyes," he said, "we were not lovers, except for one time, which was a result of circumstances that never again occurred."

I must have looked dubious.

"You see, I loved my wife very much. We were childhood sweethearts and had never been apart in our thirty years of marriage. Her four years of illness drained my heart as well as my libido. After she died, I found I had totally lost interest in sex and not even Irina's beauty and youth could arouse me." He suddenly looked surprised. "I don't know what made me tell you all this. It is, in fact, very personal and really not any of your business. Whatever came over me?"

I could have told him. It's that simpatico quality that makes me a magnet for confidences and confessions even from virtual strangers. People just tell me things and seem to feel better for it. I'm not complaining. That quality has been the cornerstone of my career. So if you've been reading my books and toying with the temptation to follow my footsteps because it sounds like such a fun profession, better ask yourself if you have been born with (it can't be learned) that special talent for bringing forth the heart-to-hearts from people.

"But you did guide and direct her," I said.

"Of course, I try to do that for all my young adherents."

Adherents! I think the man has delusions of inspirational grandeur. I had all I could take of and from him. I looked at my watch.

"I must go. It's getting late."

"Oh yes," he said with a smile, "the famous Easter ball."

"You know about it?" I asked.

"Everyone in St. Petersburg knows of it. It is the international event of the year."

He signaled for the check, which I paid. Don't come down on him for being a cheap sponger. I alluded earlier to the low salaries of Russian academics. Now let me tell you just how low. Anatoly, one of the most highly respected computer experts in the country and a full professor at the University of St. Petersburg, earns the munificent monthly salary of eighty dollars. (No, this isn't a typographical error—it's $80.) The bill for coffee and poppy-seed cake for two was twelve dollars. To give you a simpler idea of the percentage ratio between the total of our bill and Anatoly's income, think of this. If you made $2,000 a month, the cost of coffee and cake for two would be $300. How can they go out to eat then in Russia? The short answer is—they can't and don't. The long answer is—the only ones who can and do are the new Russian millionaires and the Mafia. Everyone else eats and entertains at home.

Besides, I invited him and the protocol in Europe is that the one who invites is the host. I learned that fact the hard way. On one of my first trips to Europe, I phoned an acquaintance and suggested we meet for tea at the Savoy in London. I didn't have too much money then, but I thought it would be a fun experience. She accepted with alacrity, saying, "Thank you, I'd love to." It was only when the check arrived and she looked at me with a patient smile that I realized I was expected to pick up the whole tab. She wasn't saying thank you for thinking of me, she was saying thank you for paying for me.

In this situation, however, it was not just economics that made it correct for me to treat; it was also fairness. After all, I needed him—I was taking up his time in order to pick his brains. It was only right that I pick up the tab. We shook hands and I went down to the lobby to order a cab.

"The fare will be ten dollars," said the surly man at the transportation desk, a little concession I now knew was owned by Mafia.

I knew how to say "screw you" in Russian but figured it wouldn't be politic.

"You won't get it for less," he said intimidatingly, with the confidence of a man with a monopoly.

Oh no? You've got the wrong customer, mister. I walked down the huge outside staircase and crossed to the bus stop on the opposite corner. Then, as I had seen many Russians do, I stood at the curb and held up my hand. Within minutes a car pulled up.

The driver reached over, opened the passenger-side door, and said, *"Gd'e?"* Where?

I told him my destination and said, "Four dollars."

He nodded, and off we went, and he took me safely home. I know, I should never get into an unmarked taxi. That was one of the many warnings I was given before I left for Russia. Like all the other caveats I got, it was nonsense. You have to exercise caution and use your head in any city in the world. But in broad daylight in front of a bus stop filled with waiting passengers and across the street from a huge hotel, it seemed reasonably safe to pick up one of the many cruising unofficial cabs that abound in St. Petersburg.

When I entered the house, it was six o'clock and the place was humming with activity. I went up to my room and looked forward to a nice long hot bath. But first I had to make a phone call.

I got lucky. Detective Chief Superintendent Valtonen was still in his office. I asked him about his Russian prisoner. He sounded very dejected.

"His name, we learned, is Yury Berezov. Unfortunately, he is no longer our prisoner."

Damn!

"We could not hold him since we had no evidence to tie him to the murder. He had witnesses who claimed he was at the Melodi Club all that day."

"But they're Mafia friends—they'd swear to anything."

"We know that. But the manager of the club is a respectable businessman and his word must be accepted."

"What about the gas-station attendant who recognized his car?"

"Berezov claimed he loaned the car to a friend, who, of course, swears this was so. Usually we can interrogate a suspect skillfully enough to get him confused. But this one is a tough seasoned professional and could not be moved. His lawyer insisted we release him immediately and the judge agreed. We had no basis to hold him. There is now no way we can tie him to the murder.''

So the murders of Irina and Stosh were just to be dropped from the books and the killer allowed to go free? These were not my cases and there was no one to pay me for solving them. But weren't they my responsibility? Irina may have died in place of me, and certainly Stosh died because he was with me. How could I in good conscience walk away from that?

I soaked in my bath for a half hour and decided what I must do.

I came down promptly at eight and was gratified to see a cluster of people in the foyer. It's always nice to make an entrance, especially when you're wearing a gown for which you shelled out $3,400. No matter how attractive a woman may be, she always needs the security reinforcement of outside approval, which in this case consisted of three princes applauding as I descended the staircase. Prince Oleg, his brother Prince Mikhail, and Prince Aleksei looked absolutely stunning. Tall and regal, they were in full dress, wearing white gloves and rows of colorful decorations. They looked like they had just stepped out of a Lehar operetta.

Aleksei stepped forward to kiss my hand. I know, I couldn't believe it either, but somehow it didn't seem excessive or hokey in this setting.

"Emma, you look absolutely beautiful."

I had chosen a brown satin with velvet trim by Belville Sassoon that I had picked up in Saks last month. It has but one shoulder and a skirt that wraps around from the back, leaving a large vertical opening from ankle to thigh. I didn't even try to compete with what I knew would be acres of diamond tiaras and emerald-and-ruby-bedecked bosoms, but wore simple Tiffany pavé diamond maple-leaf earrings set in platinum and eighteen-karat gold and the matching bracelet.

"Ah, the ladies," said Oleg as his wife and sister-in-law came down the stairs. Katrina looked every inch the princess in an off-the-shoulder pink satin ball gown with a full skirt. Tatyana carried herself like a queen in a deep blue long-sleeved satin gown with matching sleeveless coat that did wonders to camouflage her tendency to overweight. Both women wore diamond tiaras and elaborate diamond-and-gem necklaces.

"Come," said Oleg. "Let us prepare to greet our guests," and each gentleman took his lady by the arm and led her into the ballroom.

I gasped with delight. It was like entering an enchanted world. The ballroom was the size of a soccer field and was now aglow with huge crystal chandeliers that illuminated the carved ceiling that was ornamented with gilt stucco molding. The building had been designed by the famous Italian architect Bartolomeo Rastrelli, who in the mid-eighteenth century developed a reputation for being the greatest master of Russian rococo. His touches were evident in the complex patterns of colonnades that lined the walls, each topped with intricate gilt carvings. Between some columns were golden sconces that originally held candles and now sparkled with electric illumination. Between others were gold-framed paintings and tapestries. At the far end was a small platform which held a group of musicians who were now playing Handel's *Water Music* quietly.

"Could this be?" I asked in awe as I walked along the walls viewing the paintings.

"Yes," said Aleksei. "It is indeed Rembrandt. We have two. And a Watteau, and a Fragonard . . ." and he continued to reel off names of artists whose works I have never seen anywhere but in museums. "Thanks to the efforts of an ancestor who was a great friend of the Empress Catherine—and I mean an unusually good friend—our family came into many superb works of art. Fortunately, when he felt he was falling out of favor with the lady, he was wise enough to avoid the lady's furious and usually terminally punitive displeasure by fleeing to Paris and taking his entire collection with him."

"The tapestries are Gobelin, of course," I said, peering closely at the wall hangings.

"I guess I never gave you the full tour in this house; you've been too busy since you've been here," said Aleksei, smiling. "The library has a case filled with priceless Russian thirteenth-century icons."

"That ancestor must have been some piece of work himself to elicit all these goodies from Catherine. From what I've read, the old gal exacted heavy-duty devotion and stallion service from her beaux. Judging from his rewards, his performance must have been exhaustingly stellar. He may not have fled from her displeasure but rather from her pleasure.''

Aleksei laughed heartily. ''Quite possibly. In any case, he left his family a superb legacy. My great-grandparents were able to anticipate the revolution and in the early 1900s shipped all the treasures to a Swiss vault, where they remained until we moved into this house. Now we felt at last we could bring them home.''

''Ah—there you are, my beauty,'' said a booming voice. It was Abba, dressed in black tie, his usually free-for-all beard neatly trimmed and his fly-about hair carefully combed.

''Abba, you look positively distinguished,'' I said in delight.

He spun around to give me the 360-degree view. ''The wonders of a cummerbund,'' he said proudly. ''Look, Ma, no gut.''

''May I add my compliments, too,'' said Aleksei. ''You look absolutely transformed, Colonel. But now I must leave you to join my parents on the receiving line. I shall see you later, Emma.''

''I look transformed? From what to what? That's supposed to be a compliment?'' said Abba, fuming. ''I looked like a piece of shit before and now I don't? Or I looked good before and now I look like a piece of shit. The guy's a putz.''

''Calm down, my friend,'' I said soothingly. ''You look wonderful, as you well know, so don't start working yourself up over an offhand comment by a thoughtless person.''

He snorted. ''That wasn't an offhand comment. It was what we call in Brooklyn a left-handed compliment, the kind that makes you debate whether to thank the prick or punch his lights out.''

Just then the music changed to some Purcell trumpet music to indicate the arrival of the guests, who began to stream in. Within thirty minutes the entire room was filled with magnificently gowned, bejeweled women and men either in colorful uniforms representing the elevated ranks of royalty, or in full dress highlighted with ribbons and medals. Waiters and waitresses dressed in colorful Russian costumes circulated trays of hors d'oeuvres and champagne and the sounds of conversations in many languages filled the room with that lovely hum of people having a wonderful time. I met many people I knew, exiled members of royalty I had met either in London, Lisbon, Paris, or New York.

"Every count and countess, prince and princess, duke and duchess in the entire Western world is here,'' I said, looking around.

"Some of them probably don't have a pot to piss in,'' said Abba. "Look at all those medals. They must have emptied every fucking pawnshop from here to Hoboken. Wait till I call my mother in Florida tomorrow to tell her who her boychik was hanging around with last night. She'll be the hit of the canasta table.''

Suddenly the music changed and everyone started to move into positions.

"They're playing a *pas de span*,'' I said. "I love that dance.''

"So do I,'' said Abba.

I looked at him in astonishment. "You know how to do it?"

"Know it?" he said as he led me into the formation on the dance floor. "I was one of the stars of the Kharkov ball held on Ocean Parkway every year by the Fraternal Kharkova Society of Brooklyn. As soon as the band struck up the music, the guests would part like the Red Sea for the Becker family—that's my mother's side—to lead off the dances; we were the best Russian dancers in the entire society. First would come Uncle Zena with Aunt Genia, then my mother and me, then Aunts Nina and Jenia, and then Aunt Raya and any man she was sleeping with that week. You should have seen us—the Bolshoi Ballet couldn't have done better."

As we swung into the lineup of couples and began executing the graceful steps, he asked, "But where the hell did a shiksa from Rye learn to do such a hot *pas de span*?"

"In my senior year at college, I was a counselor in a children's summer camp called Birchwoods in Northampton, Massachusetts, run by a pair of ex-flower-children from Greenwich Village. No militaristic camp-like rules, no flag raising, no rah-rah, no competitive activities, no patriotic songs. There was folk music and ethnic dances and lots of songs with the words *freedom* and *peace*."

Abba was a marvelous dancer. He had that Zero Mostel fat man's lightness on his feet that made him seem to float over the dance floor. We were swinging along joyously and soon I noticed couples were moving behind us until we were the head of the line. Then the music stopped and everyone started applauding; they were looking at us and smiling and clapping.

Prince Oleg and Princess Katrina came over and said, "My dears, you are the hit of the ball," said the prince. "Wherever did you learn our dances so well?"

Abba and I looked at each other. "You give him the short version," I said.

"My family came from Russia, and Emma learned at college."

Katrina clapped her hands delightedly. "Wonderful!"

The orchestra struck up a waltz and we decided to sit this one out.

"Is there anything you can't do, Emma?"

I spun around. Good Lord. It was Mark.

Mark Croft, Earl of Chelmsford, future Duke of Sandringham, heir to one of the oldest and wealthiest dukedom's in Great Britain—the man to whom I was engaged to marry.

Abba stood speechless, which for him was a first.

"I'm delighted to see that you're still wearing my ring." He was looking at the antique ruby-and-diamond ring he had given me at our last meeting, at which time he agreed that my taking this family heirloom held no strings, which was the only condition upon which I would accept it.

He turned to Abba. "How nice to see you, too, Abba." Then he looked at me with a smile and said, "May I ask you to dance? I'm afraid I couldn't handle those energetic Russian things that you two just executed so marvelously, but I don't make too much a fool of myself with a waltz."

Abba waited to see if I needed rescuing. I nodded to him and walked onto the dance floor with Mark.

"How have you been?" he asked as he put his arm around me and I instantly felt that frisson of emotion that he always aroused in me. Damn, damn—was I still in love with him? If I was, would I have gone to bed with Stosh? I may be in love with Mark, but I don't feel committed to him. If I still find other men sexually desirable, does that preclude marriage to him, or is that just human? Women are supposed to require emotional involvement with whomever they have sex with, but that may be a myth or not pertain to all women. We have been led to believe that a man could love his wife dearly and still enjoy a casual roll in the hay. Isn't that also possible of women? Whenever I've been deeply in love with someone, I never looked at another man. But then we were together all the time and the opportunity never arose. I do believe in monogamy; sleeping around is promiscuity. But Mark and I haven't seen each other for a while and I don't feel any responsibility for celibacy. According to the shrinks, talking out your problems helps resolve them. I've just done that, for which I'm sorry if I bored you and you don't even get two hundred dollars an hour for listening. But if it makes you feel any better, it hasn't done a thing for me either. I still don't know what to do about Mark.

"I've missed you terribly, my darling," he said as he crushed me closer to him. "I can't believe my luck in finding you here." Then he looked into my eyes. "What are you doing here, may I ask?"

"Oleg and Katrina are old friends. I had to be in

St. Petersburg on business and they invited me to stay with them."

"Business? You are on a case?"

"Yes."

His lips tightened. He felt that my career was what kept me from marrying him. It was a pleasanter explanation for him to accept than the real fact, which was that I didn't know if I could spend my life with the aristocracy's arrogant sense of entitlement and total intolerance of those they regarded as lesser than themselves. He was dead wrong about my attitude to my career. To me, work is work and life is life. I'd be perfectly happy to give up my work for something that would give me greater satisfaction and at least an equally good income. Marrying Mark would sure as hell take care of the high-income part—he'll be one of the richest men in England when he assumes the dukedom—but I'm not convinced about the satisfaction component.

"What brings you here, Mark?"

"My parents have been friends of the Romanovs forever and have always come to the Easter ball. But my sister Caroline is expecting her first child this week and she wanted her mummy to be around, so they asked me to come in their stead. Actually, I have some business to attend to in Russia, so I was happy to oblige. A happy happenstance all around, wouldn't you say?"

"What sort of business?"

"Some sort of investment," he said evasively.

Does everyone have investments in Russia? This must be like Sutter's Mill in the days of the Gold

Rush, with everyone falling over each other to reap fabulous potential riches if they didn't die in the attempt. The reputed plethora of priceless natural resources that appear to be accessible to anyone with the cash and connections has created a free-for-all here that may well end up all smoke and mirrors.

I didn't press Mark for details—now. When the dance ended, he was leading me off the floor toward some chairs when a genial Aleksei appeared before us.

"Mark, my parents and I are delighted that you could come. I see you've met our lovely houseguest."

"Oh yes, we've known each other for some time," said Mark.

Aleksei's face took on the black look of an incipient tornado. He wasn't a guy who liked to be crossed in any way. As an only son of doting parents, darling little Aleksei had probably been denied nothing except discipline. I didn't want to give Mark any false hopes, but the temptation to torture the pouting prince was too great.

"Mark and I were an item last year; we were talking about marriage," I said sweetly.

Direct hit. If duels were still legally and socially acceptable in today's St. Petersburg, I think he would have taken off one of his white gloves and whipped it across Mark's face. Mark was too happy to notice; he just beamed and put his arm around my waist. It wasn't that Aleksei was madly in love with me; he was merely mildly smitten. But he was undoubtedly one of those kids who would never let you play with one of his toys even if he hadn't touched it for years.

"Hello, children—are we all having fun?" It was Abba who was undoubtedly drawn by the brewing brouhaha. The man has a nose for trouble and can spot it from fifty feet. Since he wasn't high on either of my suitors, I could see from his gleeful anticipatory expression that he was enjoying the clash of the titans.

"You're a real sweetheart," I said under my breath to him. "You're like those bloodthirsty creeps who go to the circus hoping to see one of the aerialists fall and miss the net."

"No, it's more like the Romans who enjoyed seeing the Christians thrown to the lions. Like them, I don't really give a shit which one loses."

Just then, the orchestra struck up an old Russian folk song called "Stenka Razin" and everybody began to sing, including me.

"You know this song, Emma?" asked Aleksei, obviously pleased.

"Yes."

"Camp Birchwoods?" asked Abba.

I nodded. "It's a beautiful but sad song. It's about Stenka Razin, who brings his adored beautiful young bride on his ship. During the voyage his devotion to her becomes apparent to the crew, who accuse him of being obsessed to the point of being unable to carry out his captainly duties. To prove to them that they're wrong, he throws her overboard."

"Typical Russian solution," said Abba. "If someone becomes a problem, eliminate her. Isn't that the way your Russian Mafia works?" he said to Aleksei. "It's part of the national character."

I could see Abba was bucking for fireworks. That

173

was not the sort of entertainment I felt was appropriate to this occasion, so I took him by the arm and said, "Abba, let's dance."

"But they're still singing," he protested.

I pulled him toward the dance floor. "I know the song, it's almost over." Of course, it had about ten more stanzas.

"What's the matter, *ahuvati*, you didn't approve of shit-stirring?" he asked as we stood in front of the musicians.

"My answer to that question is my favorite three-word question: to what end?"

"I'll respond with yet another question. What woman doesn't enjoy a little skirmish between her swains?"

"A skirmish, O.K. But this looked like we might be headed for World War III. I admit I got a certain amount of pleasure out of aggravating Aleksei, but he's not the kind of man one would want for an enemy and I don't want either you or Mark to be put into that dangerous position."

He turned serious. "Let's go outside for a minute." We went through the doors and sat down on one of the red-silk-damask-covered benches that lined the corridor.

"You met with Anatoly?" he asked.

"Yes. The man scares me."

"Why?"

"He strikes me as one of those unworldly naïfs who think they know how to run the world. Such people are annoying but usually harmless. Unless they have power."

174

He nodded. "What do you see as his power base?"

"First, he has a cadre of young idealistic followers whose minds he can easily bend. Secondly, he has that database of Mafia activities, which means he knows where all the bodies are buried. Up to now he's been totally neutral, which is why all those killers allow him to operate and merely regard him as innocuous. I think they're wrong and at any moment, when he's ready, he plans to use all that information and Lord knows what other data he's accumulated covertly, the most frightening being his possible knowledge of where the Soviet nuclear materials are stockpiled."

Abba looked at me admiringly. "Are you sure we can't recruit you into the Mossad? You could be one of my star *sayonim*."

"Thanks, but I have no desire to be part of your international network of civilian volunteers. The cause may be just, but the price isn't right."

He shook his head sadly. "So beautiful and yet so mercenary. Does money mean that much to you?"

"Damned straight it does. But what does all this have to do with the Mossad?"

He sighed. "Do you really think I'm here in St. Petersburg solely to watch out for your cute ass or that I've been hanging around just to attend the Easter ball? We know about Anatoly and we're worried that some of that nuclear material can be sold to terrorists and countries like Syria and Iraq, who would like nothing better than to blast Israel out of existence."

"Why don't you, to use a nice euphemism, just neutralize him?"

He laughed. "You've only been here a few days and already you're thinking like a Russian."

"How wicked of me. Of course you folks at the Mossad are pacifists."

"We haven't eliminated him because we need him to tell us where the materials are. The locations are undoubtedly in his computer. We've had everyone from teenage hackers to computer geniuses trying to break into his system and it's invulnerable—so far."

"What a country this is," I said. "Everything is for sale. I'm waiting for some Texan to buy the Hermitage and have it shipped stone by stone to Dallas. I wonder what sort of investment Mark is into here?"

Abba was surprised. "His dukeness has dipped his aristocratic toe into this cesspool? That ought to be worth buying tickets for. His upbringing hasn't prepared him for the scumbuckets he'll have to deal with here. They don't know from 'a man's word is his bond' and all that 'gentleman's agreement' honor shit. They'll ream his royal ass for sure."

"Mark is tougher than he looks, Abba. Besides, anyone investing in Russia at this time is motivated by pure greed and deserves all the financial punishment he may get. Now let's go back in. I want to dance."

"Right—I think I'll find myself a princess or two to twirl around the floor."

I found Mark looking for me and we spent the rest of the evening in each other's arms. It was heavenly. When supper was announced, we headed for the dining room and he observed Abba squiring a princess on each arm.

"Your friend certainly has a way with women."

"I know. He doesn't look like Sean Connery, but he seems to convey much of the same animal magnetism," I said fondly.

"You like him a lot, don't you?"

"I love him," I said simply. "I would trust him with my life."

"I think I'm jealous."

"Don't be. Abba holds a special position for me that is unique and therefore doesn't conflict with any other relationship I might have."

"Are you saying, then, that you and I have a relationship?" he said hopefully.

"But, Mark, of course we do."

He sighed happily. "Great. Let's eat."

The dining room looked like a fairyland. The tables were covered in yellow with centerpieces made of lilies and Easter eggs. Along the walls on each side of the room were long buffet tables manned with servers dressed in colorful Russian costumes. We got on line behind Prince Michael and Princess Marina of Greece and their daughters, Princesses Olga and Alexandra.

I looked around the room. "Many of these royals are more accustomed to standing on the other side of the serving tables. A lot of them work as waiters. Having a title doesn't entitle you anymore to a lavish stipend and free room and board."

We took our plates to the nearest table. Other guests soon joined us and within minutes, Mark became engaged in conversation with an old friend of his who was seated on his right.

"May I join you?" It was Dmitri Thomasov, the skater.

"Of course, Dmitri. Sit down, please. How nice to see you. How is everything?"

"The practicing is fine. But it has gotten a lot noisier and busy around there."

"What do you mean?" I asked with interest.

He shrugged. "They are hammering and banging next door in the factory, and bringing in new equipment. There is constant activity. They seem to be fixing up the place."

"Are you perhaps going there tomorrow, and if so, can I hitch a ride again?" I asked quickly.

"Yes, I am going and I would be delighted to have your company."

I barely noticed what I ate. What's going on at the Tsvetnuye Metalluy and why are they making improvements now? I was so preoccupied that Mark had to shake me.

"Darling, they're doing their *pièce de résistance* now. You must watch."

The lights dimmed and from four corners of the room came a parade of waitresses carrying candlelit trays of *pashkas,* the traditional Russian Easter dessert. We exclaimed with delight as one was placed in the center of our table.

During dessert, the entertainment began. Russians enjoy performances while they dine and every Russian restaurant features them. As usual, it consisted of a troupe of spirited dancers in colorful folk costumes who screamed and played balalaikas as they whirled around banging tambourines and other noisemaking devices. Colorful as all get-out, but hardly the kind of background conducive to tranquil dining. You can eat during the show if you don't mind the agitation to your digestive system and the inevitable damage to your clothes, since it's almost impossible to watch the performers and your dripping soup spoon at the same time. And you sure as hell can't converse. Abba came over to sit at our table during the entertainment. A troupe of Cossacks came onstage and began waving their sabers as they performed the *kazotsky* and other energetic dances. I noticed Abba sat still while everyone else clapped and cheered at their antics.

"Why aren't you applauding? They're terrific," I said.

"I should clap for Cossacks? Those anti-Semitic motherfuckers used those sabers on my grandparents in pogroms at the shtetl."

I sighed. "Abba, get a grip. They're not real sabers and they're not real Cossacks. They're just some starving dancers who are probably being paid ten dollars each to entertain you. You won't be betraying your ancestors if you applaud their talent."

Suddenly he noticed Dmitri. "Isn't that . . ."

"Yes, the Olympic skating champion I told you about. I'm driving out to Lomonosov tomorrow with him." And I told him why.

He shook his head solemnly. "I don't like it. Be careful."

IX

I WAS ASTOUNDED. The building that when I last saw it looked like an abandoned factory was now a respectably active plant. The windows had been washed and broken ones replaced. All debris had been removed, the entire place looked neat and reasonably clean. I opened the newly repaired and painted front door and walked up to the front desk, where the same receptionist was still manicuring her nails. She didn't bother to look up at me or acknowledge my presence in any way. They had improved the building but not the attitude of the personnel. If near starvation and high unemployment hadn't changed their work habits, it could take a generation.

"I would like to see the manager," I said in Russian.

Cynthia Smith

"Who are you?" she asked, barely glancing up from her busy emery board.

"I am a writer doing a story on the new Russian industry," and I flashed my ASJA membership card, which shows I am a paid-up member of the American Society of Journalists and Authors. It's an organization I joined some years ago as an auxiliary member so that I'd have the card to flash for just such occasions as this. The identification of a writer is one of the best entrées almost anywhere in the world. Not only does it explain your interest in whatever place you're visiting, but it gets the respect usually accorded to creative people.

That got her, as usual. Right away she was envisioning herself on the cover of *Cosmopolitan*. She sat up and actually smiled.

"I would like to interview your manager."

She picked up the phone and I heard her paging him. Good sign. They have a functioning paging system. Within minutes the phone rang and she explained my request. Five minutes later the plant door opened and a burly, short man in shirtsleeves emerged.

"Can I help you, maybe?" he asked in heavily accented English.

"Da, pazhalsta." Yes, please.

He looked relieved when he heard my Russian. *"Ah, gavariti parushka. Kharasho."* You speak Russian. Good. "What can I do for you?"

I told him my story of having an assignment from an American magazine to write about the resurgence of Russian industry and how his revitalized plant

182

looked like the perfect example I sought. He beamed with pride. I had pushed the right button. He invited me into the plant and my stunned reaction when I walked in made him beam even more. The place was humming with activity. No more idle machines, no more dawdling employees, every piece of equipment was in use. The floors were swept and potholes repaired. All this accomplished in four days. Apparently, when properly motivated and financed, things can get done efficiently and quickly.

I knew where the financing was coming from, but what was the motivation? I found out after my interior tour with the manager was completed and I left the plant to inspect the exterior.

"Good morning."

It was Vladimir Nickonov. Right behind him was Yury Berezov. There are times I almost regret not carrying a gun; this was one of them. Abba has always tried to persuade me to carry a weapon and I refuse and always will. Violence begets violence. I am not in law enforcement, I am not a policeman, I am not even a private eye. The argument is to be armed in order to defend yourself. I have always been able to accomplish that with words and my brain. Of course, there's always the possibility that a situation will arise where they won't be effective. I hoped this wouldn't be it.

They both stood there just looking at me impassively.

"Good morning," I answered with a smile. Sure I was scared, but why should I let these fuckers know that?

Cynthia Smith

"Do you want me to kill the *pizida* now?" asked
Berezov.

I tried not to show anger, which would show I understood that one profanity that makes me livid. *Pizida* means "cunt." He was smiling with the kind of
eager anticipation that did not bode well.

Needless to say, I waited rather impatiently for the
answer.

"*Nyet*. She's unimportant—just a nosy *manda*. But
she's a good looker. I wouldn't mind if she would
otsosi," he said in Russian with a revolting leer.

It was good I didn't carry a gun or I might have
shot both of them where they lived—in their crotches.
He called me a nosy cunt and said he would like me
to give him a blow job.

"You are here with your skating friend again?"
asked Nickonov in English.

"Yes. I was admiring how nice the plant looks.
Amazing what a little soap and paint will do." I
smiled. "Bye-bye," and I turned my back and walked
away toward the rink. You must admit that took real
cool. A little ways down I turned around; they were
still standing there watching me. I waved and continued walking. It was only a five-minute walk, but it
felt like an hour.

"How did the practicing go today?" I asked Dmitri
as we drove back to St. Petersburg.

"Quite well," he said.

"I hope it went as well as the little charade you
played to get me here today," I said calmly.

The car swerved a bit. "Take it easy, Dmitri. It's
not worth killing both of us."

"How did you know?" he asked.

"After that chilling encounter with those two Mafia goons, I realized they were expecting me and put on that whole little act for my benefit. I was lured there for the specific reason of seeing the work in progress at the plant. You had to be the one."

He pulled the car off to the side of the road and turned to me. He looked dreadfully upset. "They told me they would kill my children if I didn't do what they asked. I got myself invited to the ball so that I would meet you. They told me what to say that would interest you to come to Lomonosov, but if not, I was to invite you and get you out here."

"Did they tell you why they wanted me here?"

He shook his head.

"You realize they may have wanted to kill me?" I asked softly.

He nodded and looked down. Then he lifted his head and I could see the misery in his eyes. "But my children. What could I do? You don't know those beasts," he cried. "They have no mercy, no hearts. They murder women and children as easily as you would swat a fly."

I looked at him with compassion and felt an intense hatred toward the ones who destroyed good men like Dmitri. He would suffer guilt and might never forgive himself. But what choice did he have?

Mark was waiting for me at the house when I returned. I found him in the sitting room with Oleg and Katrina, having tea, of course.

"We had a date for dinner," he explained, "so I

thought I'd come by a bit earlier and pick you up for cocktails. I guess I should have phoned.''

"No matter," I said. "I see you're being well taken care of. It won't take me but a few minutes. I'll just go up and shower and change."

"Why hurry, my dear?" said Katrina. "Join us for a cup of tea. You must be weary after your trip. Lomonosov is quite a distance from here. We do so enjoy chatting with you, but you always seem to be flitting off somewhere or other. Perhaps I shouldn't say that; after all, you are a professional woman and undoubtedly have many important things to do. Me, I am just an idle woman and don't really understand the pressures of time you busy folk have," she said with a gracious and gentle smile.

"You, idle?" said her husband with an indulgent smile. "With all your meetings and charities, I think you work harder than most executives."

She looked sad. "There's so much difficulty here in St. Petersburg and so many people needing help, one must do what one can."

I looked at Mark. "What's our schedule, your lordship? Do I have time for tea?"

"Absolutely. Our reservation is for eight, so relax."

"Great!" I flopped into a chair. "I'd love a cup of tea but no goodies," I said, looking regretfully at the cake tray. "Dmitri and I stopped for lunch at some charming place along the way and I've already consumed my calorie allotment for the day."

"You were with the skater?" asked Mark.

"I watched him practice; he's marvelous. He's sure to take gold at the next Olympics."

"We hope so," said Oleg. "We are very proud of him in this country."

We chatted pleasantly and after a while I excused myself and went upstairs. Taking my cue from the gray tweed jacket and fawn trousers that Mark wore, I chose a black-and-red Ungaro suit, black Manolo Blahnik shoes, and my black Prada bag.

"You look charming, love," he murmured as he took my arm. "As always."

The restaurant was elegant, but I didn't realize how elegant until I opened the menu.

Bear Steak—$99.

"Is this an error? They mean rubles, don't they?"

"No, madame," said the waiter. "All prices are in dollars."

"Catching a bear must be extremely labor-intensive," I said with a straight face.

"Not to mention the need for outrageously costly weapons and ammunition," said Mark.

As we looked at the ludicrously high prices on the menu, we began to giggle.

"Ten dollars for a cup of borscht?"

"How about fourteen dollars for a glass of Louis Jadot red wine? In New York, a full bottle costs about half of this."

"Shall we go?" I asked Mark.

"No, we shall stay. It's only money and I have so much it's almost vulgar."

"You mean I could order the bear steak?" I asked.

187

He hesitated. "Well, my darling, I can afford it, but I must say I abhor being taken."

"Never fear," I said. "There are certain animals I will accept on my dinner plate—and bear isn't one of them. I never order rabbit either because I used to raise them as a child and I make it a practice to never eat anyone I know socially. I'll have the beef Stroganoff."

It was actually a lovely place with the welcome change of entertainment being provided softly by a string quartet. We were able to enjoy our conversation. I asked how his political career was progressing, and he grimaced.

"I think it's going splendidly, but I'm afraid Mother doesn't share my opinion. She thinks things are moving far slower than they should. She doesn't seem to understand that these things take time."

"They speak of the impatience of youth," I said. "But it's actually the old who are impatient and justifiably—they have fewer years to wait for things to get done. Your mother is in her seventies I imagine, and she wants to see you prime minister in her lifetime."

He nodded.

"I see you're not protesting the possibility. Does that mean the party actually has you on the P.M. track?" I said in surprise.

He nodded again. "Yes. It may sound immodest, but the powers that be seem to think I should be groomed for the top job. Right now I'm slated to run for a seat that's coming available in Leeds. In fact, I've just bought a place in Ripon as a base."

"Mark, I think that's wonderful, if that's what you want and aren't doing it just to fulfill your mother's ambition."

"I believe it is what I want—but what I really want is to have you at my side always," and he reached for my hand and looked at me lovingly.

This is the point where romance novelists say, "She felt her heart do a flip-flop."

They very well may be right, because I felt something going on inside, but I couldn't swear which organ was reacting. For all I know, it may have been my gallbladder. There's no doubt that I have feelings for Mark, but are they strong enough to make me willing to alter my life so drastically? Time to change the subject.

"How do your business interests fit in with your politicking?" I asked. That was a pretty neat segue, don't you think?

"It's been rather hectic but I enjoy the activity," he said.

"What sort of business interest are you involved in here?"

Appropriate timing in your questioning makes the difference in being regarded as interested rather than nosy. I'd been dying to find out what he was really doing in St. Petersburg and here was the perfect opening.

"I've become interested in a small computer company. It's run by an absolute genius, a man who is one of the most famous theoretical computer visionaries in the world. He's a professor of computer science at St. Petersburg University."

"Anatoly Yakolov," I said.

He was amazed. "You know of him?"

"No," I said. "I know him."

"That's absolutely marvelous. You see, everyone knows him." he said enthusiastically. "Did you know that he creates concepts that are so advanced and avant-garde that there are maybe only ten people in the world he can talk to, who comprehend what he's saying?"

"Perhaps on some levels, but he's transparently clear on others," I said. "Are you planning to back him in some specific venture?"

"Quite right. He has come up with the most incredible advance in computers that will knock the world on its ear," he said, his eyes dancing with excitement. "It's a device that allows you to have your E-mail instantly translated into any language in the world."

"That does sound fantastic," I said. "Exactly how does it work?"

"It's comparatively simple. You type in your E-mail, double-click on a translation icon, and then type in what language you want it sent in. Your recipient immediately gets your message—in his language."

"That's incredible," I said. If it works, I thought. I hate people who puncture other people's balloons. "Have you seen it in action?"

"Of course. I'm not a total ass, you know. I would not be putting a million pounds into a project that I didn't see proven beyond a shadow of a doubt."

A million pounds! Why am I getting visions of

Anatoly driving around Switzerland in a new Mercedes?

"Tell me about the demonstration," I said with starry-eyed interest. Skepticism at this point would only turn him off. I want the whole detailed picture and I wouldn't get it if he were on the defensive.

"I brought a French computer expert with me who, of course, knew of Professor Yakolov. At his laboratory, two computers had been set up. We watched one of his assistants type in an E-mail letter in English, click on French, and it immediately appeared on the second computer totally translated. My expert checked the language and it was indeed word-for-word correct. It was incredible."

"What questions did he ask the professor?"

"He asked him how the software can understand signals of a humongous selection of many languages. Anatoly explained everything and then put the computers through translations into ten other languages. When my expert asked, 'What size is the reference cache?'—meaning how large is the repository—the professor answered, 'Not quite as large as we would like it.' That was the ultimate convincer." He looked at me triumphantly.

"That was a good answer?" I asked.

"Of course. It is the correctly modest answer of a true mathematician or scientist who is never fully contented with his work. It validated his project."

"What was the assistant's name?" I asked.

He looked surprised. "He was introduced as I remember, as Genek something or other, I'm not entirely certain. There was a young woman there, too—Galina, I believe.''

The whole crew. Either the professor had convinced his disciples to work purely for the privilege of serving the guru, or there would be three Mercedes and Swiss bank accounts on the horizon.

"The way I see it," said Mark excitedly, "there's an endless potential for the product. The UN, for instance. Anatoly says the next step will be to make it voice-activated instead of requiring messages to be typed. Can you just see every delegate with a monitor in front of him on which appears, in his own language, the instant complete translation of the speaker's words instead of the edited version he gets now through his earphones? Think of the difficulties and crises that could be averted. Emma, I tell you the possibilities for the professor's creation are mind-boggling.''

"How did you meet him?" I asked. How did you get so lucky? I thought.

"Through Countess Irina. I came over here a few months ago on business and ran into Aleksei and his cousin at one of the restaurants in the Hotel Astoria. I mentioned I was weary of handling real estate—I manage all the family properties, as you know, and I would dearly love to be able to subsidize some enterprise that would bring benefit to the world at large, and not just my family. Irina said she knew a professor who was doing some marvelous work which might interest me. She arranged a meeting and, well, I was sold. I understand the poor girl was murdered just last week. What a tragedy.''

"Anatoly must be deliriously happy at getting the money, I expect."

"Well, actually, he hasn't received a sixpence yet. The papers are being drawn up and you know lawyers, they take a lifetime to dot the *i*'s and cross their *t*'s. I've been trying to rush them, but who can ever hurry a lawyer?"

"They're just doing their job of protecting their client."

He laughed. "Oh dear, forgive me. I forgot I am assailing your profession and colleagues."

"People love to make their lawyers into whipping boys when things don't turn out as they would have liked. The guilty criminal blames his lawyer when he doesn't get him off. The businessman who cheated on his taxes claims his lawyer did a bum job when the judge sentences him to ten years in Allenwood. But should the accused be acquitted, he attributes it to his own innocence. No one gives his lawyer credit for saving him from a bad deal. And that's what your lawyer is trying to do. Let him take all the time he needs to design a loophole-proof contract."

The longer the better. Of course, the whole thing would be an exercise in futility, because a contract is only as good as the characters of the individuals who sign it. I'd bet Anatoly hadn't bothered to engage a lawyer since he didn't intend to even read the contract because he had no intention of honoring it. Am I being cynical? Let's test my theory.

"Negotiations and contracts take a long time, Mark. After your lawyer draws it up, then Anatoly's attorney has to examine it."

He smiled. "Oh no, we won't have to lose that much time. Anatoly says he doesn't need a lawyer because he leaves all those business details to me."

There are times I really hate to be right.

"He says he's just a professor, not a businessman, doesn't understand those matters, and will gladly sign whatever I come up with. He trusts me implicitly. Isn't that rather charming?" he said with a smile.

That wouldn't be the word I'd choose. "I think your lawyer should be given all the time he needs. After all, you expect this to be the beginning of a major enterprise. People starting a business are always impatient and think all they need are a few pages to cover the current start-up operation. But a lawyer knows that the business could grow and he wouldn't be doing his job if he didn't provide for all the exigencies that might arise in the future."

He looked a bit dubious. "Well, I am a bit impatient because I heard Genek mention to the professor something about another potential investor who wants to get in on the project. I don't want to lose out on this opportunity, Emma."

Cripes—they didn't miss out on a single trick. Do they give a course in old St. Petersburg U on "How to Catch and Con?" The first lesson must cover how to give the prospective schmuck the old squeeze play until he's panting with desire. I knew there would be no point in trying to disenchant Mark at this point. For one thing, I had no facts to back up my suspicions, just my assessment of the situation and of the character of the professor. Delaying tactics were my only chance.

"Mark, may I ask you a favor?"

"Of course, my darling."

"When you receive the contract, may I look it over just to give it my seal of approval? I have every confidence that your solicitor is excellent, but I've done so many of those kind of deals that I may just notice some missing points."

He looked at me with a tender smile. "How sweet. I love that you want to protect me. Of course I promise you will see it before I give it to Anatoly. There—happy?"

"Ecstatic. But please let this be our little secret. I would prefer that no one know that I have any involvement in your business."

"You have my word."

I'm never quite clear on time-zone differences, but when I got home that night, I called my friend Bill Yates in Cupertino, California. I knew there was a nine-hour difference between Russia and New York. I don't know if I ever mentioned it, but I'm mathematically illiterate and am paralyzed by numbers. When I call information for a phone number, by the time I've heard the end of the message, I've forgotten the numbers the operator gave me at the beginning. (Note: to the people who are bothered by my self-confidence, which they consider bordering on smugness, I hope this little confession about my shortcoming will make me a little more endearing.) So how could I figure out what time it was in California? The hell with it. Bill is a good enough friend to not complain too bitterly if I should be awakening him in the wee hours of the morning or creating coitus interruptus late at night. Bill and I went to Rye High School together lo these many years ago. He was the class nerd computer nut. He didn't walk around with a pen holder in his shirt pocket nor did he wear bottle-thick glasses like the classic Hollywood nebbish. But his choice was to spend prom night in his room play-ing with his computer rather than with his friends in the ballroom of Orienta Beach and Yacht Club. Bill Yates was a computer genius whose only regret is that he was only one letter away from being the richest, most brilliant computer guy in the world.

I told him the Anatoly story and asked about the viability of his product.

"Sure, it's a great idea, which is why we've all thought of it. Unfortunately, the technology to accom-plish it is about ten years away, and for the voice-activated part, probably fifteen years. I know Anatoly. I've met him at symposiums and conventions. Just six months ago, in fact, at a seminar at Stanford. He's highly respected for his computer knowledge but not for his character. He's one of those guys you never discuss your work with for fear it'll turn up on a paper he'll be presenting at the next convention. As far as developing any major breakthrough, the Russians are big on brains but almost nonexistent on technology. We get all their people out here because they're leav-ing Russia in droves. Who would want to stay in a country where scientists make in a month what a su-permarket checker here gets paid in a day? And those glorious white nights they rave about only mean more hours to contemplate the disintegration of their build-ings and the squalor of their homes. I've spoken to

Anatoly and I'm sympathetic to his strong desire to remain in his homeland. I think I'd be reluctant to leave my roots, friends, and family. But I've heard him talking to some of his countrymen who have settled here, at UCLA, Cal Tech, and Stanford, and I've seen his face when he hears their salaries and sees their luxurious homes and two cars in the driveway. The guy's obsessed with making money. He's crazy to be rich. Given that voracious greed and somewhat indifference to ethics, I wouldn't trust him as far as I could throw a mainframe. Tell your friend to run, do not pass go, and do not collect two hundred dollars.''

I thanked him and we chatted about the old days and old friends.

"How are your mom and dad?" he asked. "I always thought they were sort of cool."

All my friends envied me my parents. In the seventies, when drugs and cults were the raging attraction for teenagers, many parents tried to keep a tight rein on their kids. Not my mom and dad. Totally sanguine that they had done a good job of instilling responsibility in their child, they gave me total freedom. No curfews, no edicts. I had their total trust and I never violated it.

After I hung up, I got a yen to talk to my mom and dad. It was April, so they were still in our house in Rye. They spend winters in their condo in Florida, and fall traveling. Did I tell you it was my parents who taught me the value of money? Not just making it but the all-important pleasure of spending it.

I dialed their number. Please don't think I'm one of those outrageous sponger houseguests like the

Duke and Duchess of Windsor, who were renowned for making calls to around the globe without offering their hosts a penny's compensation. I use my phone credit card, of course.

"Hi, Mom. It's Emma."

"I know it's you, darling. I have only one child, so no one else calls me Mom."

Did I tell you my mom is a pistol?

"Where are you calling from, Emmy Lou?" said my dad, who had apparently picked up the extension, to my mother's evident chagrin. Since he retired two years ago, she bemoans the fact that her private life is no longer private. Whenever the phone rings, he's there in a shot to listen in until he's satisfied that he knows the reason for the call. It drives my mother batty. All her friends, most of whom have similar difficulties with newly leisured husbands, have learned to start off their calls with graphic complaints about their vaginal difficulties, which gets the guys off the phone fast.

As for that name my father called me—Emmy Lou is my baptismal name, after some super-feminine piece of southern fluff relative of my father whom he hoped I would grow up to emulate. Right. I changed it to Emma the first time I saw Diana Rigg play Emma Peel in the wonderful English series *The Avengers,* and now the only person permitted to use that dreaded name is my dad.

"I'm in St. Petersburg, folks."

"Florida or Russia, dear?" asked my mom.

"Russia. I'm staying with Prince Oleg and Princess Katrina."

"Wonderful. Do send them our love, sweetie." They had all met when the Romanovs were staying at my apartment in New York last year.

"Is this vacation or work, honey?" asked Dad.

"Work," and I thought, Boy, is it ever.

"It's April—Orthodox Easter," said my mom. "They must be having their famous Easter ball soon."

"Last night, Mom. It was gorgeous, as usual."

"Who was there?" she asked avidly.

I'm a good daughter—I recited the list of luminaries slowly so that she could write them down as I knew she would, in order to fully regale her friends over the bridge table tomorrow.

"And what did you wear, dear?"

I gave her a full description of the gown, the designer, where I bought it, and how much it cost—in other words, vital information without which her presentation would be incomplete.

I gave them all the details of my trip to Helsinki—well, not quite all. When I told them I had seen *Boris Godunov*, Dad asked if they did it with the Rimsky-Korsakov score. He explained to me that the opera is usually performed from the score prepared by Nicholai Rimsky-Korsakov, who revised the opera in 1896 and again in 1908. The score as Moussorgsky wrote it was published by the Soviet government in 1928. As you can see, my dad is a true opera buff and is the one who gave me the love and understanding of that marvelous form of musical art.

I told them Abba was here with me, which pleased them; they're also crazy about him. When I mentioned the presence of Mark, I could hear my mother's swift intake of breath. She's one of those great mothers who never pushes or pries, but I know she's dying to have me marry the future Duke of Sandringham. I didn't mislead her with any false hopes, but just enough info for her to know the possibility was still alive and she could still tell her friends that Emma was dating a duke. I'm a good kid and try to bring my folks pleasure whenever I can. Lord knows they were knocked for a loop when I abandoned the prestigious and secure law profession for a wild-sounding precarious career as a Private Resolver. Since they had spent a small fortune for my law-school education, they were entitled to question my choice. But not a peep out of either of them. I once thanked them for their lack of interference and they both looked shocked.

"But, dear, we felt we brought you up to have good sense and good values. We think we've done a pretty fair job and you've turned out quite satisfactorily. Now the rest is up to you. We love you and trust you and will always accept whatever you do."

Now, if that isn't a model for the perfect parental attitude, I don't know what is.

"When do you think you'll be back home in Rye, honey?" asked my dad. "You have to see my new bird feeder that I set up in front of my study window. I'm getting cardinals, blue jays, redheaded woodpeckers, chickadees—it's great. I sit at my desk and watch them. I call it 'Nature's television.'"

"He's going absolutely bonkers over the thing," said my mom. "He just signed up to join a bird-watching group at the John Jay Marshlands Conservancy.''

"It's a helluva lot better than golfing," he protested. "You used to complain that eighteen holes took me all day. A bird-watching walk only takes an hour or two."

Bird-watching! Of course. I said my hurried love and good-byes and phoned Helsinki.

"Detective Superintendent, you said you had no witnesses who saw Berezov in Hanko. Talk to the bird-watching group. They are at the beach in the morning and early evening. I saw them that morning. I'll bet Berezov was with them in the evening. Bird-watchers are fanatics—he would not have been able to resist such an opportunity."

I got the callback two hours later.

"There were twelve watchers in the group that evening. We gave them your description of Berezov and every one of them confirmed he was there."

"Yippee! That ought to do the bastard in. Have you started extradition proceedings?"

"What for? We picked him up an hour ago at the Melodi Club. An ordinary criminal would have escaped to Russia immediately. But the Mafia are so arrogant that he felt perfectly safe staying in Finland. I assume he feels we'll never be able to convict him because he will pay off the witnesses."

"Would he be able to do that?" I asked.

"I would say his chances are remote if not nil. One of the bird-watching witnesses is the mayor of Hanko and another is Miss Leena Nurmi, the town librarian. They are both firmly committed to their identification.

Bribing witnesses is a common occurrence in Russia. But Finnish people take their civic duty extremely seriously. That would never happen here. And just another point. When arrested, he was found to have a stiletto knife on his person, which we shall compare with the victim's wound. If it's a match, we have him. Miss Rhodes, I must thank you for your help. If we can ever aid you in any way, please feel free to call upon me.''

"There is something you can do."

"Name it."

"Allow me to sit in on your interrogation of the suspect."

"You mean observe through a one-way window?"

"No, sit in the room and participate in some of the questioning."

He was silent for a few seconds. "It's highly ir- regular, but under the circumstances that we wouldn't have him in the first place if it weren't for you, and you are a professional, I think we can make an ex- ception. Can you be here tomorrow morning?"

"I'll be there."

I caught the morning plane to Helsinki and was in the police headquarters building by eleven. I was greeted in the lobby by Rikos Komisario Vuori and given an ID badge. She brought me upstairs to the interrogation room, which—she corrected me—they called the interview room. It sounds so much less threatening, don't you know, and I guess it's sup- posed to make the suspect feel more comfortable and thus less guarded. But one look at the stark gray walls, plain brown metal table, and the policeman leaning against the door and you know you're not there for a manicure. Berezov was seated with his arms folded. Those deep sunken Georgian eyes registered nothing, but when I walked in, his face produced a rictus that I realized was a sneer. I repressed a shiver—this is not the sort of guy you like to have as an enemy. The interpreter, a young blond man, was seated on one side of him and his lawyer on the other. Across the table was Detective Chief Superintendent Valtonen, who was conducting the interview in Finnish.

I sat quietly observing Berezov, who from time to time would look at me. I could see that he wondered what I was doing there but was aware that I was a threat. At one point he looked at me and said something in Russian to the attorney, who quickly said, *"Astanaviti!"* Stop. I couldn't get the entire statement because he spoke softly, but I gathered the lawyer told him to shut up because you don't know who in the room speaks Russian. Good point—smart lawyer.

At first, Berezov stuck stolidly to his alibi—he was never in Hanko, he was in Helsinki with friends all the time. A policeman came in and whispered something to the superintendent.

"We're ready for the lineup now."

A few minutes later I stood in the room with the one-way mirror and watched a group of loutish-looking men with numbers on their chests standing against a lighted wall. Berezov was number three. Six people were called in one by one to pick out the man they remembered having been with them bird-watching in the early evening on the day Stosh was murdered. One after the other unhesitatingly picked out number three.

When he and his lawyer heard the results of the identification parade, the lawyer began to waver, but Berezov looked scornful.

"Who cares what a bunch of *mudacks* say!"

Although we knew that *mudacks* means "motherfuckers," the superintendent and I remained impassive and waited patiently for the censored translation.

"These idiots, as you call them, are the mayor of Hanko, the town librarian, and four councilmen."

The lawyer exclaimed and his client began to show the first signs of nervousness.

"By the way," said the superintendent. "You might want to know that I have already spoken to RUOP and they agree that extradition is out of the question, since the crime occurred on Finnish soil, which gives us positive jurisdiction."

"I would like some time to talk with my client now," said the lawyer.

"It's time for tea anyway," said the superintendent. He turned off the tape recorder and we walked out, leaving the two of them alone in the room.

It was the perfect strategic time for a break and I could see the superintendent was pleased with the progress of the interview.

"I speak Russian fluently, but I find it expedient not to reveal that fact to prisoners," said the superintendent. "You'd be surprised what information I pick up that way." Wouldn't I, though?

"Berezov wants to be sent back to Russia because his Mafia group has strong ties to the police, unfor-

tunately, which means he would be freed at once.
Now that he knows that's out and his phony alibi
would never stand up—what Finnish court would
take the word of some Russian hoodlums over the
testimony of twelve upstanding Finns?—this is the
time to let him stew and accept the realities of his
situation."

I was delighted. It looked like that monster would
be punished and stopped.

"Now, what did you wish to talk to him about?"
asked Valtonen.

I told him about Irina's murder, which was committed the same way as Stosh's.

"You want to ascertain if he did it? All right, but
I think it would be best if I handle it. After all, he
has no obligation to answer your questions and his
attorney has a right to refuse to allow him to answer."

"I have no problem with that," I said. "I'm very
impressed with your interrogation technique."

"Thank you." He flushed with pleasure. "We may
not be the New York Police Department, but we attend international seminars on law-enforcement methods and we're not the country bumpkins you might
think."

I sensed that he would be uncomfortable with compliments, but he was selling himself short. He was
damned good. There's a certain amount one can learn
from training sessions, but interrogating prisoners is
a complex undertaking. It requires an innate understanding of psychology and keen insights that cannot
be taught. Every suspect is different and must be handled individually, and you have only a few seconds

to make the decision about what approach will be the most effective. The old "good cop, bad cop" style has been too overdone on television to have any effect today. A good interrogator must be creative and make up his own techniques as the situation changes.

When the interview resumed, the lawyer was acting conciliatory and the suspect looked shaken. Gone was the smug smirk; he no longer felt invulnerable.

Valtonen sat back in his chair sipping tea. His attitude was friendly, conveying the feeling that now that the matter had been somewhat resolved, we could all relax.

"Do you enjoy the ballet?" he asked casually.

"Da," said Berezov tentatively, uncertain of where the conversation was going.

Valtonen maintained that offhand attitude, as though they were two friends chatting. He nodded with an approving smile, as though pleased with their shared tastes.

"Yes, so do I. Especially the Kirov. They are magnificent. Have you ever seen them do *Sleeping Beauty*?"

"Da." Berezov was now completely relaxed, basking in the approval of his inquisitor.

"Great, wasn't it? I would have loved to attend their eight hundredth performance last week. Probably you would have, too, but I understand tickets weren't available for the likes of you and me. Only for special VIPs and rich people."

"I was there," said Berezov proudly.

"You're a fortunate fellow," said Valtonen admiringly. Then, without missing a beat, in the same calm amiable voice, he suddenly switched to Russian. "Then you must have seen that bit of trouble that happened near Prince Aleksei during intermission."

Before realizing what was happening, Berezov answered, *"Da."* Not having to wait for the translation, he had instant comprehension and thus answered by reflex. When he understood what he had just done, he turned brick red and looked murderously at me. Suddenly his lawyer became aware that something was amiss and started to protest and direct his client to button his lip.

I had what I wanted. I got up and walked out of the room with an impassive face, but let my emotions cascade when I got outside. I wanted to squash this vermin who had killed beautiful young Irina. I felt gratified that my suspicions had been correct. But most of all, I wanted to get the person who had given the orders that shortened the vital life of a lovely young woman.

When he emerged from the interview room, Valtonen assured me that Berezov would be punished for Irina's death, though not specifically. He had no doubt that he would be convicted of Stosh's murder and would surely receive the maximum sentence under Finnish law. I was feeling vindictive and was unhappy that there was no life imprisonment in Finland, which means the miserable bastard would be out in sixteen years max. He cold-bloodedly destroyed two young people I knew and Lord knows how many more. I wished the creep had committed his crimes in France and I entertained visions of me knitting happily as I watched the guillotine come down on his neck. However, I'd have to be satisfied with the fact that he'd be locked away for some time and no longer present a danger to society. But I wouldn't be totally satisfied until I knew who the real villain was—the person who ordered him to kill.

X

I HATE TO talk to clients while working on a case and I never do, except in mercy situations. Like when the clients were anguished parents whose son was purported to have committed suicide.* I specifically do not ask for up-front retainers because that would entitle them to bugging rights, and if there's anything an investigator hates, it's the time-wasting nuisance of dealing with demanding clients who call you at will—theirs. However, I needed to talk to Ellis Brannock now in order to achieve a specific end, so I took a deep breath and dialed his private number.

"Where the hell have you been?" he exploded.

I sighed. It was the kind of reaction I expected. Clients who are ordinary mortals are miffed that I

*Impolite Society

don't keep in touch with them. Imagine how men who have come to believe they are gods because no one ever denies or defies them would react to being ignored.

"Have a nice day yourself, Ellis," I said brightly. "And how's the family?"

He quieted down a bit. "What's going on?" he asked. "I expected a phone call from you days ago. You owe me that."

"My dear Ellis, since you haven't paid me a nickel, I owe you squat. When I took the case, I told you my terms, among them being that I don't do progress reports. I consider them a time-wasting pain in the ass. When I accomplish my mission, I give my clients a comprehensive review and they give me my fee and we bid each other a fond farewell."

"O.K., tough lady. Then to what do I owe the honor of this call?" he said. His voice was a mixture of amusement and respect. I imagine no one had spoken to him that way in twenty years.

"I visited the Tsvetnuye Metalluy factory the day after I arrived and it looked like a crack house in the South Bronx." I described the conditions graphically and I heard his swift intake of breath. "But had there been any valuable working machinery in the place, you wouldn't have had to worry about theft, because the place was secured by a couple of tough Russian Mafia guys who acted very proprietary about the entire operation—as though they owned it."

"Son of a bitch!"

"However, take heart, Ellis. I was there yesterday and my visit seemed to have done wonders. The place has been resurrected, refurbished, and generally spruced up. They knew who I was and what I was actually doing there. The last time I was there they didn't, probably because I got to Russia too quickly for the informant to alert them to my coming. It usually takes some days to get an entry visa to Russia and whoever it was didn't figure on Ellis Brannock's power to kick ass when it came to bureaucracy. Who was the whoever? Obviously someone advised them who I represented and they set me up for a return visit so that I would send the message home that all is well.''

''And you want to know who advised them of your identity.''

''Right.''

''What do you want me to do?''

''I want you to pull the chain of the guilty party. You realize that someone on the board had to set up this arrangement with the Lomonosov Mafia. I'd like you to attend an emergency board meeting, which you should call for tomorrow. Then tell the happy band of campers everything I've told you—but with an addendum to my tale: that I know the identity of the board member who masterminded the joint operation.''

''Then I expect you want me to check the underwear of everyone on the board?'' he said with grim humor.

''If we're getting into toilet humor, I want the culprit to be hoisted by his own petard, exact translation from the French meaning suffering from one's own fart, *péter* being the French word for breaking wind.''

''It's so educational having a Sarah Lawrence graduate investigator,'' he said with a hearty laugh. ''I must interject that piece of arcane wisdom at my wife's next dinner party. It's those little tidbits that give one the reputation for erudition and wit.''

''Or for being a tasteless boor. I'd check with your wife first if I were you. She may not share your sense of humor.''

''You're right. Unfortunately, I found out too late that she doesn't share my sense of anything.''

''She's quite young and beautiful, I hear.''

''True, but alas, neither trait has lasting value. And sure as hell are boring to live with.''

''Good. I'm always pleased when rich older men who trade in their wives for younger models get stiffed.''

''You're right. And I've done it twice. Will I ever learn?''

''Not until you come to accept that the aging process comes to all men, even rich ones, and that marrying a young wife doesn't fool the grim reaper.''

''Thank you, Gloria Steinem,'' he said. ''O.K. I'll set up the board meeting right away.''

''I'll be back in a few days. That should give the alleged perpetrator enough time to sweat.''

''Ah, you want him, or her, to make the mistakes nervous amateur criminals inevitably commit.''

''What makes you think they're amateurs? The way I sized them up, not one of your jolly board of Santa's helpers reached their exalted position without developing an expertise in chicanery and double-dealing. However, even pros become rattled when they smell trouble. The difference between them and amateurs is their solutions tend to be more elaborate—but often no more effective."

"I bow to your superior knowledge, Ms. Rhodes. While you're working out whodunit, I'm going to enjoy choosing my method of retribution for the son of a bitch who has been fucking me over."

"Public flogging is no longer fashionable, Ellis. And though I know you think you're a law unto yourself, methinks you'd best have the real law handle the matter."

When I hung up, I had the distinct feeling that he would ignore my advice. What made me uncomfortable was that Ellis Brannock had a reputation for demanding loyalty and taking vicious retaliation against those who were disloyal to him. Powerful men like him get to believe they are Tefloned against punishment for their actions. I didn't think he'd end up in Attica, but that was his problem—as long as I collected my fee first.

There was a knock on my door. It was Abba.

"How about going out for a glass of tea, *tsotskele*? There's stuff to talk about."

We found a small café right off the Nevsky Prospekt and took our tea to a corner table. He listened carefully as I recounted the results of my trips to Helsinki and Lomonosov, and about Mark's involvement with Anatoly Yakolov.

"O.K., that cocksucker Berezov has been removed, but killers are like cockroaches here, they multiply overnight. Nickonov's KGB background gives him connections that make Berezov's elimination a mere bagatelle. He's undoubtedly been replaced already.''

"Still, it's satisfying to know that a killer is being punished and being put out of commission," I said.

"It's the professor who interests me at the moment," he said thoughtfully. "With an enterprise as elaborate as he's planning, he has to be involved with Mafia. I've known the guy for years. He's a tech genius but a schlemiel at business. He runs a little software shop where he designs great things for clients and then forgets to bill them. His credit is turned off regularly because he loses suppliers' invoices. Mark may be a bit of a tight-ass, but he doesn't strike me as a fool. He had to have seen some sort of proposal and spreadsheet before he agreed to back the project. Somebody had to prepare the documentation. That's were the Mafia came in for sure.''

"They do that sort of complex accounting?"

"Are you kidding? The have staffs that make Coopers and Lybrand look like my cousin Max the CPA. They're highly sophisticated and I imagine Anatoly turned to them for help. Knowing the total Mafia networks, he had to know the right one to approach, most likely Stosh's. They were special friends, plus the fact that Stosh's organization was geared for technical business.''

"But the professor didn't need tech help; he and his acolytes would provide that. He and his nefarious proposition would be welcomed by a *gruoppirovka* like the one in Lomonosov, who could be looking to

build up their technical-industry clientele. That's it!"
I nearly shouted.

"What's it?" asked Abba. "You look like you just
got one of those big-time epiphanies like I got when
I realized that wontons and kreplach were identical,
which proves a Sino-Judaic affiliation that is validated
by the number of Chinese restaurants you find in
every Jewish neighborhood."

"We've been looking at this backwards," I said in
great excitement. "Anatoly didn't go looking for a
Mafia connection—they came after him. The Lomonosov gangsters now needed their own technical
expert and he was it. His whole plan was probably
worked up with them; it's too complex and grand in
scope for a limited man like him to have cooked up.
Stosh was killed not because the Lomonosov Mafia
were afraid his group was getting ready to take over
the Tsvetnuye Metalluy but because they plan to become the major player and had to deactivate the competition."

"Holy shit—you're right." He gave me that rueful
admiring look I'm getting used to seeing whenever I
come up with a brainstorm.

"No, I do not have any Jewish blood. We've been
pure unadulterated WASPs for generations, and although your people are admittedly generally smarter
than the average bear, the condition is not exclusion-
ary."

"So you're not only a brilliant analyst, you're a
mind reader, too?" he said with a big laugh. Then he
turned darkly sober.

"If you're right, and I think you are, there's going

to be a range war in the near future just as soon as Stosh's group locates a replacement. It's easy to find another piece of shit like Berezov but a Cal Tech–trained computer scientist doesn't show up every day in the week. They'll have to go on a recruitment search and that takes time, but when they find him or her, it'll be *High Noon* time and everyone better clear out of town and leave the bloody streets to them.''

''I think they're going to have another decimation in their ranks soon.''

Abba looked at me questioningly. ''Who?''

''Someone in their group had to be the mole who notified Nickonov that Stosh was going to Hanko to pick up his car. I'll bet Berezov wasn't in Helsinki just by chance. He was probably sent there to follow us.'' I shivered.

''That *kus-amack* really gives you the creeps, eh?'' said Abba. ''I feel the same way. People who kill for a cause may sometimes be misguided, but they're not immoral because they believe in something. But those who kill for pay and pleasure like Berezov are the lowest forms of humanity, if they're human at all.''

We both sat drinking our tea quietly. There was something very disquieting about this whole country these days, and I hoped it didn't become a permanent condition. It was just this kind of widespread depravity, despair, and lawlessness that pervaded post–World War One Germany and led to Hitler. The major difference here and cause for hope was the nation's vast natural riches and the extensive foreign interest and investments.

''What am I going to do about Mark?'' I asked.

"Marry him," said Abba. "You'll be Mrs. Prime Minister someday, besides being one of the richest women in England."

"I'm not talking about my love life, I'm talking about Mark's actual life. If I convince him to withdraw his support for the professor's project, there's a chance they may kill him."

"Not if he's out of the country when he notifies them he's pulling out. And you, too. You think they won't know who axed their fucking deal, sweetie? Get his ass out of here and yours, too."

I knew he was right. Which meant I needed to do a little planning.

I phoned my friend Cissie Henderson in New York. We had both been art-history majors at Sarah Lawrence, to the degree that our school had majors. Most people do not know that Sarah Lawrence is a unique-in-America college that follows the Oxford University style of education where students pursue independent study programs guided by one-on-one tutorials with their professors. The school does not have the usual rigid requirement curriculum which frequently forces students to take courses in which they have no need or interest. It demands one of the highest number of books to be read and reports to be written of any school in the country and provides a magnificent well-rounded education for the self-motivated individual who functions on his or her own without the need for disciplined direction.

Our art-history professor despaired when I entered law school, but much as I loved the field, the pragmatist in me couldn't overlook the fact that there was really no crying need for curators in a country where maybe ten people out of a thousand go to museums, whereas everyone at some time sues or thinks of suing someone. Cissie, however, didn't have to concern herself with practicalities since she came from a lineage of robber barons who made their millions in the days before taxes and such inconveniences as antitrust laws. She started her career with the Metropolitan Museum in New York with the considerable advantage of knowing everyone who had a billion or over, and rose to become one of the best acquirers of collections and donations the Met had ever seen. These days she has her own business using her elite connections and persuasive manner for fund-raising for any institution that could afford her very expensive services.

"Emma, darling—from where are you calling? Zambia? Alaska? Or some other exotic spot that your audacious career takes you?"

"I'm in Russia—St. Petersburg. First let me tell you why I called and then we'll get to the 'what's doing' details. I hate when people call and go through an inane chatty preamble they feel is mandatory to which I'm not listening because I'm trying to figure out what the hell they want."

She laughed. "That's so Emma-ish. No bullshit. Cut to the facts. Go, I'm listening."

"What kind of benefit affair could you throw if I give you three stellar guests of honor: the Earl of Chelmsford and future Duke of Sandringham, and Prince Oleg and his wife, Princess Katrina, of the Royal House of Romanov?"

She gasped. "Are you kidding? They could outpull Brooke Astor, Caroline Kennedy, and Fergie put together. I've been looking for a way to raise money for My Sister's Room, a home for abused women. With your fabulous royal threesome as the lure, I'll have no problem in getting a sponsor. This would open up the deep pockets of every social climber in New York, especially the self-made moguls with brand-new trophy wives who have everything they want except the two things money can't buy—social acceptance and class. I can start a marvelous bidding war between Perelman and Trump for the best table."

"Great. I'll guarantee the earl. You invite the prince and princess. I assume you'll offer to pay their fare."

"Of course. Non-reigning nobility is the second cheapest group on earth."

"Who's the cheapest?" I asked.

"Reigning nobility. Prince Andrew not only demanded a first-class round trip on the Concorde, but the royal suite at the Plaza plus a week at Disneyland."

"There's one catch."

She sighed. "I knew it was too good to be true. Do they all insist on my bringing over their entire domestic-staff retinues?"

"No. It docsn't involve expense, just timing. I need your gala affair to be held this week."

"Whew! You scared me. That's no big deal. In fact, it can be even better," she said excitedly. I could hear her fertile brain working.

"I'll get someone to donate her town house; they'll

be falling all over each other to be asked. Then all invitations will be made personally by phone instead of mail. Far more chichi. And the guest list will have to be limited, of course, due to the smaller facility. They'll be flattered to death to be the chosen ones. It will be the most prized invitation of the season!" she said triumphantly.

"Great! I'm here at Oleg and Katrina's home. I'll drop a little hint how exhausted the poor things look after the tremendous strain of putting on the Easter ball. Then I'll suggest they need a break and why not come and stay with me in New York. They'll balk at the fare and your propitious call will clinch the deal. I'll provide the ground arrangements, you'll provide the travel arrangements. It can't miss. Phone tomorrow to give me a chance to bring up the idea tonight. Your call will seem positively fortuitous or a God-sent omen if you're Orthodox. Do you think you can get a sponsor and a confirmed date set by tomorrow?"

"With those drawing cards, all I'll have to make is one phone call. O.K., now that our business is settled, let's get to the personal. I hear the young earl is real dishy. Your positive assurance of his presence tells me there's something going on between you two. Either you're blackmailing him about some sort of kinky naughtiness, or he's hot for your body. Or could it be that you've snared one of the best catches in the world today since John Kennedy, Jr., got married—and he's too young and callow anyway."

"The problem is I've snared him, but I'm not sure he's snared me."

"You mean he's talking the big M-word and

you're vacillating? Emma, love, have you lost your mind? You're thirty-five. Not only is the biological clock ticking away, but so is the marriage one. Guys of our age are not looking for women of their age: I see them in this week's hottest SoHo and TriBeCa restaurants with girls whose breasts stand at full attention without visible means of support. Soon all you'll be eligible for is the position of third wife for some tycoon whose resentful children are older than you are and whose sperm are heading for the last roundup. You've got a man who's not only within our age range who can give you little dukes and duchesses but is also handsome and rich. Emma, come home. I'll have to knock a little sense into you. You're in dire need of a reality check."

XI

ROYAL EXPATRIATES LEARN early the value of their titles and how to exploit them in return for all kinds of freebies. I knew it would be fairly easy to convince Oleg and Katrina to come home with me since it was just the kind of offer they have never refused.

I was glad Aleksei wasn't joining us for dinner that evening since he might want to be included in the deal, which was a complication I didn't need.

"Darlings, the Easter ball was a fantastic success," I said. "But it's taken its toll. You poor things look absolutely weary, but I'm not surprised—it took a horrendous amount of work and you did a wonderful job."

Actually, neither one lifted a hand except for writing the check to the caterers. Their experienced staff took care of everything. I've met many women who throw huge parties that are handled totally by competent and hugely expensive caterers and spend the next day in bed accepting the accolade phone calls from friends who compliment them on their competence for hosting such a smashing success. "Darling, you're simply marvelous. I don't know how you do it what with your hectic schedule," which consists largely of lunching and shopping. As in all such situations, the only difficulties Oleg and Katrina had to endure was the inconvenience of keeping out of the way of the caterers, which they felt entitled them to feel justified in accepting my compliment and commiseration.

They both looked in the pink, but wilted appropriately before my eyes.

"I have an idea," I continued. "I insist you both come back to New York with me for a week. You can rest, away from all your responsibilities here, and also visit with old friends. You'll stay with me again, of course. I promise you, Maria and Francisco will take excellent care of you."

I had brought that wonderful Portuguese couple home to New York after their Vila do Mar employer was sent to prison, thanks to my efforts.* They needed a job and I needed a couple to take care of my New York apartment when I'm elsewhere and take care of me while I'm there.

Katrina looked at Oleg. "It does sound wonderful, dear, don't you think?"

*Impolite Society

I could see he was dying to accept, but the cost of the fare was holding him back. "I don't know, my love, perhaps I'd best talk it over with Aleksei. Where is he?"

"I believe he said he had some business to take care of at his stables and probably won't get home until late."

"His stables? You mean he owns them, Katrina?" I asked.

"Of course. They are in Pushkin. He is an excellent horseman," she said proudly.

Oleg frowned. "He spends a lot of time with those horses," he said petulantly.

"But, darling," she said soothingly, "you know they're part of his business. Remember the money he made a few months ago when he sold one of his horses for a huge profit?"

Most likely Oleg wanted to discuss the trip to New York with Aleksei in order to hit him up for the airfare. I needn't worry about Aleksei's reaction since Cissie's call tomorrow morning should settle the matter.

"Look, you two, you needn't give me your answer right now. Although I'm planning to go home to New York tomorrow or the day after and it would be nice if we could travel together."

O.K., they're pretty much in the bag. Now to deal with Mark. After dinner, I phoned his hotel and fortunately found him in.

"Darling, how great you called. I just got back from a meeting with Anatoly and I'd love to see you."

He sounded exuberant. Damn. "How about the bar of the Astoria in a half hour?" I asked.

"Capital!" he said.

I hung up before he could think of suggesting I come to the bar at his hotel. I didn't want the inevitable "let's go up to my room" aftermath that might interfere with the success of my mission, which was to get him to agree to come with me to New York and attend Cissie's gala.

After we ordered brandy and sodas, he started talking excitedly about all the promises and projections Anatoly had laid out for him. Only my years of listening to misguided clients' "sure-thing deals" stopped me from exploding with a barrage of piercing questions that would expose the unrealistic ramifications of Mark's dream. There would be no point in doing that now.

"Mark, I'm going back to New York tomorrow or the next day."

His face fell. "So soon? I thought we would have more time together."

"I have to get back to New York to settle my case. Then I'll be free as a bird and we could spend all the time in the world together." Then I looked at him with a smile. "It would be lovely if you could come with us."

"Who is 'us'?" he asked.

"Oleg and Katrina, I hope. They're going to be guests of honor at an important fund-raising event being run by my friend Cissie Henderson." I looked at him wide-eyed. "Oh Mark, it would be wonderful if you would agree to be another guest of honor. If Cissie's handling it, the cause must be important and worthwhile and you would be an important contributor to the success of the event. Cissie was worried that Oleg and Katrina will draw only the dwindling senior-citizen upper crust of New York. She was bemoaning the fact that she was anxious to attract the younger set who are, after all, the future of all charities. Couldn't you please come?'' I looked at him pleadingly with the ''fluttering eyelashes'' look that usually never fails.

''Darling,'' he said, reaching for my hands. ''Of course I'll come. You know I would do anything for you.''

But this time it's me who's doing for you. I leaned over and kissed him. ''Thank you.''

We parted at one in the morning, filled with happy anticipation—he with the pleasure of us being together, and me with relief at hopefully leaving Russia in an upright position rather than in a body bag.

The next morning I took the *electrichka* to Pushkin from the *Vitebsky Vokzal* (Vitebsk Station). This is a popular tourist destination usually reached by excursion tours, the kind of trip that shows you more than you care to see, tells you details you never need or want to know, forces you to spend an hour at a souvenir-selling shop, and compels you to spend hours with people you hope never to see again. But then, that's my opinion. Since the majority of travelers prefer this form of seeing another country, I'm willing to admit there may be something I'm missing here. Nobody's perfect.

In czarist times, Pushkin was called *Tsarkoye Selo* (czar's village). It was the vacation spot for the aristocracy who wanted to be near the royal family, who spent summers in the Catherine Palace. When I arrived in Pushkin, I went to look at this dazzling building, which is the big tourist attraction and a fine example of Russian Baroque. I must confess I didn't bother to go inside because I didn't have the time for sightseeing and I had already seen the apex of this lavish architectural style in the Hermitage. If I should have the time later, I would like to stroll through the lovely park with its 1,500 acres of woods, ponds, and pavilions.

The stables I was seeking were located near the palace. Since it was the only one in Pushkin, it was not too difficult to find. It was a huge sprawling place that looked like an extremely well-run and well-kept enterprise. I was impressed. I headed for a stone building that appeared to be the offices and found two people inside.

"Dobrae utra." Good morning, I said.

"Can I help you?" said the woman seated at a desk.

"Yes, I was looking for a place to board my horse."

The man seated at the other desk looked up. "What kind of horse?"

"A seventeen-hand Hanovarian bay gelding. I use him for dressage and pleasure riding."

Are you impressed? Don't be. Half the teenage girls in the suburbs fall in love with horses; it's the classic psychological transference and preamble for boys. Every stable had its share of young tomboys hanging about, including me.

He smiled and arose. He was a tall, grizzled man

wearing a work shirt with a heavy roughly knit sweater and brown pants. Only the young in Russia wear jeans.

"Yes, we would have a place for him. Would you like me to show you around?" He wiped his hand on his pants and held it out to me. "My name is Leonid Tygunov and this is my wife, Anna." She smiled displaying one gold tooth.

I was surprised at his affability. My short stay so far in Russia had taught me to expect surly responses to every inquiry. Unlike capitalist countries where people in selling positions are taught to be, if not helpful, at least pleasant, the help in Russia don't give a damn. The old slogan "the customer is always right" has been replaced with "caveat emptor"— buyer beware. In the shops, it's actually the salesclerks who are the people of importance. Customers are only the nuisances who bother them with demands for merchandise they don't have.

I smiled back at him. "Yes. I assume you have boxing stalls roomy enough."

"We have the best and finest of everything," he said proudly.

He led me into the cobblestoned courtyard which was lined with stalls. I saw at once that there were about forty stalls, all made of fine wood. It was a nice sunny day, so many of them had blankets and sheets hanging on the doors. When I peered in, I noted that each one was deeply bedded with straw, with buckets of feed and water in the corner.

"Why the water buckets?" I asked. "I see you have automatic waterers."

He grinned ruefully. "Like everyone and everything in Russia, they haven't worked in years."

We both laughed. The one endearing trait of Russians is their ability to mock themselves.

"With Russian weather, much rain and snow, we must exercise our horses much of the time indoors," he said as we walked up to the huge indoor ring. The ceilings were very high, and the place was immaculately maintained.

"And this is our tack room," he said. It was a large room with rows of gleaming brass-trimmed bridle racks. Door handles and hinges were also brass. This place had obviously been built by someone who had deep pockets.

"I see you are looking at the excellence of the construction. These stables were built for the last Czar Nicholas in the days when the royal family came here for the summers. Of course, no expense was spared. When the communists took over, this became a place where the commisars and the KGB kept their horses because this is the finest stable in the area."

"Who owns it?" I asked.

"Me and my wife," he said proudly. "It had been in my family for generations. It was my ancestor who cared for the czar's horses."

Well, well.

We walked back to the office and he was stopped a few times by young grooms with questions. When we returned to the office, I asked casually, "I thought I might find Prince Aleksei here."

Mrs. Tygunov looked down at a schedule on her

desk. "Not today. His hours are twelve to five, three days a week."

"His hours?" I asked in surprise.

"We would like to have him more hours, he's very good with the horses, but the way things are today, we could not afford any more."

"I know Aleksei loves horses," I said with a smile.

Mr. Tygunov nodded. "We board and train some of the finest, most expensive horses in Russia," he said. "Aleksei is the only one of my workers who I allow to handle the real cream of the crop."

I heard loud voices outside and two short, heavyset men came in arguing loudly. They were obviously well on their way to being totally blotto and reeked of vodka, the liquor that boozers have convinced themselves has no aroma.

"Give us a couple of horses," they asked rudely.

I waited for Tygunov to deny them angrily since alcohol and horses are a bad mix and a sure prescription for disaster. To my surprise, he obediently went out toward the stables with the men staggering along after him.

Now I knew who really owned the stables.

"Mafia?" I said to the woman, who sat there with a grim expression.

She nodded angrily and spat out, *"Pizduks."* Bastards.

"But men in that condition can't handle horses," I protested.

She nodded and them smiled with satisfaction. "Especially the ones Leonid will give them."

• • •

THE THIRTY-MINUTE TRAIN ride back to St. Petersburg gave me time to consider the possible inferences one could make about the situation I had just discovered. Had Aleksei told his parents he owned the stables? Or did they know the truth and just want me to think he did. Why? If the stable story was horseshit, if you'll pardon the play on words, did that also apply to his fabled business interests? And if so, what did he do every day when he wasn't mucking horses and from where did he get his money?

When I got back, Abba had just come in and he immediately suggested we go out to lunch. If he was turning down the opportunity to have one of Raya's gargantuan kasha-laden meals that he adored, and which had the extra plus of being free, he must have had some serious talking to do.

We went back to the Literaturnoye Café. Over a bowl of *solianka*, he told me he was returning to Israel later that day because his mission was completed.

"You mean you've located the nuclear material?" I asked. "You've cracked the professor's computer?"

"No—we cracked the professor. He finally confessed that he's a crock of shit and made up the whole story about knowing the sites of all the silos and nuclear stuff."

"You're kidding! Didn't the wise professor realize that professing to know such critical information put him at deadly risk?"

Abba shook his head. "The guy's such a power-starved putz he just enjoyed being pursued by the entire Western world. What the schmuck didn't realize is that when the Eastern world gets into the act, tactics change. They don't plead, they just treat your nuts like lights on a Christmas tree—they turn the current on and off.''

''What happened?''

He laughed. ''Some of the *schmatte*-headed brethren detained him for questioning for an hour or two. When they weren't happy with his answers, they began to get busy with his snappy little three-piece set down below. I hear it took him all of twenty seconds to confess that his whole shtick about knowing where the nuclear bodies were buried was a fucking hoax. Unfortunately, the towel heads didn't believe him right away and he had a bad time until they finally realized they were dealing with a pathetic schmuck-brain instead of a big-time mastermind. Oh well, hoaxing can be hazardous to your health.''

I laughed.

''What the hell's so funny?'' he asked.

''I always found it amusing the way men grimace and squeeze their legs together in obvious discomfort whenever they hear or talk about unpleasant genital activity. I had a friend who gave up marrying the Jewish woman he loved because, even though he was circumcised, he was told that conversion to Judaism required a symbolic slight slash of the scrotum.'' I laughed. ''There you go again!''

''Don't you women cringe when there's talk about rough handling of your privates?''

''Abba, when men hear the word stirrups they think of horses. They've never visited a gynecologist's office, and let's change the subject.''

I told him of my visit to Pushkin.

He shook his head. "No one shovels horseshit for a hobby. He obviously needs the money. So where the fuck does our noble sonny boy get the rubles for those Savile Row suits he wears? I don't think I've seen him in the same one twice."

"It is indeed a puzzlement," I said. "But it's just another of the little mysteries I'll undoubtedly clear up when the royal couple come for a visit."

I told him about Cissie's and my plan and he grinned broadly.

"Beautiful. What a plan. You women are even more devious than the Mossad."

I bowed. "Thank you, thank you. I consider that a high compliment."

"Why are you inviting the prince and princess over anyway?" he asked.

I shook my head. "It's just a hunch I have."

"Then go for it. I believe strongly in hunches. Believe me, they've saved my life many times. It's something to do with Brannock's foundation?"

"Yes."

He didn't ask another question but just said simply, "Good luck, *ahuvati*. My money's on you, as always. When did you intend to tell Mark about how he's been played for a mug?"

"As soon as we're safely in the U.S."

"Not before," he cautioned. "Sure as hell not on the plane."

"Why not?"

"Because there are weird acoustics in an airplane cabin. Haven't you ever noticed that you can often hear clearly the conversation of someone two rows away and not catch a word from the person next to you? You never know who can pick up on what you're saying, so the rule is to avoid confidentialities on a plane.''

We chatted for a while and then left together, kissing good-bye in front of the restaurant. As always with Abba, we were both aware that we didn't know when or if we would see each other again.

XII

WHEN THE FINNAIR plane touched down in Helsinki, I sighed with relief as we awaited our connecting flight to New York. I thought we might never make it out of St. Petersburg. Princess Katrina is from the days of traveling by ship and hasn't acknowledged the baggage limitations of airplanes. She has learned that steamer trunks are no longer acceptable, but sees nothing wrong in packing an equivalent amount of belongings into four large Louis Vuitton valises. (The prestigious battered old LV luggage, not the shiny new stuff owned by any parvenu with cash.)

"My darling," Prince Oleg had said as the servants began loading everything into the waiting taxi. "We are only going for one week."

"Yes, I know, dear," she answered sweetly, "but the weather in New York can be so chancy."

I looked at the gorgeous sable coat she carried on her arm. "Katrina, it's almost May. It's much too warm in New York for that."

I realized that admonition alone would not deter her. I knew what would. "You only see frail elderly ladies wearing full-length furs in the spring."

She handed it immediately to the maid and we managed to get to the airport at the last possible moment. I had dreaded delays caused by Russian bureaucracy but had forgotten the Russian response to authority. Oleg took charge with an air of unquestionable superiority—he was the aristocrat dealing with his serfs—and the airport personnel almost bowed us through. We flew first class, of course, so it was easy for them to receive the special treatment to which they felt entitled. Even so, the four flight attendants ended up rushing back and forth to serve their needs, which I felt was all to the good since it deprived some of the slobbering businessmen of their fourth brandies. You may marvel that I was willing to give up a flight home on Ellis Brannock's private plane and pay for a first-class fare. Surely you jest. Since I was the prime mover in bringing Cissie her valuable guests, I had her pay my fare as well as theirs.

She met us at the airport with a limo, of course. The gal had style and she knew her customers. She curtsied when I introduced her to the princess, which made Katrina flush with pleasure—I don't think anyone had curtsied to a Romanov since 1917. She greeted Mark with an intensive once-over that made him comment to me later that she looked at him as though she was evaluating a horse to qualify for Ascot.

Francisco and Maria took immediate charge of my elderly guests and saw to it that they had tea before they took to their beds for an extended nap. Mark, Cissie, and I sat in my living room drinking sterner stuff.

Mark looked around approvingly. "Your home is lovely as I knew it would be," he said as he admired the Hepplewhite tambour writing table and the two chairs flanking the fireplace. "These chairs began life in France some centuries ago, I would guess. And these small bronzes seem to be of the Italy of the Cinquecento."

Cissie clapped with delight. "A man who knows his antiques. Mark, if you weren't obviously otherwise occupied, I think I might consider marrying you."

"And what would you do with your husband du jour?" I asked.

"Do what I've done with all the others, my sweet. Dump him."

"I gather you're not into long-term relationships," said Mark with a smile.

"I don't have a single relative who has had fewer than four spouses. I think it may be genetic."

"It might be curable," he said.

"Too late for me. I'm on husband number three now. How about your family?"

"My parents have been very happily married for forty years and there's never been a single divorce in our family."

"Good Lord," said Cissie. "How utterly quaint. What happens if they get tired of each other after a number of years?"

"It's all in the attitude," said Mark. "These antiques have become more beautiful and valuable as they age. We think people are the same way."

"Emma, grab the guy—he's priceless."

I smiled and sipped. "I'm thinking about it."

Mark walked over and kissed me.

Cissie beamed. "I'd love to throw the wedding. I think I could sell at least fifty tables."

We roared. "Cissie, you're incurable. You have a mind like a cash register."

"Speaking of that crude stuff called money, we're positively rolling in it from the special gala I've set up for my three royal stars. Mark, you'll surely go to heaven for agreeing to be a special guest."

"Who is sponsoring it?" I asked.

"The Ellis Brannock Foundation."

I nearly jumped out of my chair. "Who did you work with over there?" I asked.

"Martina Albertson, an old buddy of mine. She contributes her cosmetics as favors for all my parties. I called her to ask for my usual goodies and she offered to have the foundation back the entire affair. I was delighted."

"I thought they only gave money to foreign companies in countries just coming out from under the yoke of dictatorship, I believe is the way they phrase it," I said. "Why would they be interested in backing an event that raised money for an American charity?"

"That's what I thought." I know the raison d'être

of every foundation in New York; it's my business. But Martina said they're now going to change the thrust of their mandate. Actually, they'll be going in much the same direction, only the venue will change to the United States.''

Ellis must have given the board the rough side of his tongue, although I think that's the only kind he has, and scared them shitless. This new out-of-Russia policy indicated that someone was making a rush for atonement. Who? Tune in tomorrow, folks.

Cissie got up. ''Well, darlings, I must be off. I have about a million things to do. I'll send a car for you tomorrow; it'll be here promptly at seven. The town house is actually just ten blocks away on Fifth Avenue and Seventy-fifth. Wait until you see who'll be there,'' she said triumphantly.

Mark got up and kissed her, excused himself, and headed to the bathroom.

She looked after him. ''He's positively dishy. If you let this one slip out of your hands, Emma, you ought to be certified. And what a draw. All the younger new-money set are dying to meet him. Not only because he's titled and has probably played doctor with Princess Anne, but he's going to be one of the richest men in England. They're intrigued with royalty, but they worship only one thing—money. As for Oleg and Katrina, they've pulled in all the older generation of big givers. Emma, my love, I owe you one.'' And she left.

Mark walked back into the room. ''I didn't really have to use the facilities, you know,'' he said. ''I just felt you two girls undoubtedly had words to exchange that could only be said without my presence.''

"How did you know?''

"I have a sister, remember?''

"How is she?''

"The baby hasn't arrived yet. Mum and Dad are still sweating it out.'' He looked at his watch. "I think we're both getting a bit weary and there's a big day tomorrow.''

"Would you like to stay for a bite here?'' I asked.

"No, thank you. I think I'll go to my hotel and have a room-service sandwich and Scotch and then sleep. I have an appointment tomorrow morning with our lawyers here, so I will need all my faculties. Tomorrow will probably be busy with business all day. So why don't I appear here tomorrow evening at six forty-five?''

He arrived on the dot, looking absolutely gorgeous in formal wear that fit him as though it was made for him, which of course it was. Many men look uncomfortable in dress clothes and show it by tugging at their collars or cummerbunds, but Mark wore his clothes with the same casual elegance he displayed in tweeds.

"What?'' I said in mock horror. "No orchid corsage? My escort to my junior-high-school prom brought me one.''

He looked at my strapless Valentino yellow silk ball gown. "I'm sorry I didn't bring one. It would have been rather fun trying to find a place to pin it.''

Prince Oleg walked in leading his wife and Mark and I applauded. They looked absolutely splendid. He was in uniform with a breast covered with decorations. She was stunning and regal in a full-skirted Givenchy violet satin ball gown with a large décolletage covered with a breathtaking necklace of amethysts and diamonds that matched her tiara. I made a mental note to have her put her baubles in my wall safe.

"I think they should recall the Russian monarchy," I said. "It would enrich the drab existences of the citizenry to see pageantry featuring folks like you on television. Certainly more inspiring than all those fat men with the badly fitted bulging suits and their unfashionable pudgy wives."

They smiled in pleasure. "Maintaining a monarchy can be a tremendous expense, as Mark well knows," said Oleg. "I don't think our people could afford it at this time."

"It would be far less costly than the Mercedes, graft, and corruption that they're paying for now. And a helluva lot more entertaining," I said.

Francisco came in to tell us our car had arrived.

The town house was one of the larger private homes on Fifth Avenue and one of the few that boasted a ballroom. When we entered, guests were swarming all over the downstairs rooms and even some on the wide staircase. Since everyone knew everyone else, being on the same list of fund-raiser desirables, they were all engaged in animated conversations, drinking champagne, white wine, and cocktails being circulated by tuxedoed waiters and waitresses, and munching on the familiar hors d'oeuvres they had come to expect from Glorious Foods, this year's favorite caterer. The problem with this homogenous socializing is that the menus become boringly predictable, but then nobody comes to these affairs for the food.

"Darlings, you're here. And on time, thank heavens." Cissie came swooping toward us. She eyed us professionally. "And looking absolutely perfect." She took Oleg and Katrina on each arm. "Come, let me introduce you. Mark darling, come along."

Mark looked at me ruefully. "This is where I fear I'm expected to perform like a pet poodle. But then I suppose that's what I'm getting paid for," and he followed Cissie obediently.

"Good evening, Emma. You're looking lovely tonight."

It was Ellis and the entire Brannock board. I had stipulated to Cissie that they be invited. Obviously, Ellis wouldn't spring for tickets for spouses; there were none visible. I'm never surprised when millionaires display petty chintziness. It seems to give them some crazy sort of satisfaction to cut down on nickels and dimes. Maybe it makes them feel less profligate when they buy ten-million-dollar yachts. Edsel Ford was known for insisting on making the rounds of his mansion every night to check that all lights were off.

"Well, the benefactors. Imagine my surprise when I found out we were the sponsors of this lovely affair."

"The decision came while you were in Russia," said Richard Wrigley nervously.

"Does that mean we're out of there entirely?" I asked.

"Well, that kind of depends on what you tell us,

doesn't it?'' said Red Wilkens with a big smile. ''We're all real keen on knowing what you found out about how our little old colored-metals enterprise is doing.''

''This isn't the time or place for a report, Red,'' said Bill Ephram.

''No, of course not.''

''We're having another board meeting next week,'' said Bill. ''You'll be notified of the exact time and day, Emma. You might be interested to know that we've suspended all payments to the Tsvetnuye Metalluy until then.''

''You pronounce it very well, Bill.'' His accent was perfect.

He smiled. ''The original family name was Efra-movich. Like many others, the name was shortened at Ellis Island.''

''Martina, you look marvelous,'' I said, ''and so slim.'' She looked quite elegant in Dior's dark green evening suit. She flushed with pleasure. ''Well, I did drop some pounds—but I think it's the suit.''

''I didn't realize you knew Oleg and Katrina,'' I said. ''They're old friends of mine.''

''Yes, Katrina was the guest of honor at my company's twenty-fifth anniversary gala last year.''

I'll bet Katrina didn't do that for just the fare. As I said earlier, exiled royals have learned by necessity to pull every possible buck out of their titles. A good many of them, Oleg and Katrina included, had wealthy childhoods and grew up to find they had no money and no training to make any. They had to exploit whatever personal assets they had. But then, don't we all?

When dinner was served, the honored guests were seated at the sponsor table, except for Mark, who was seated among the youth group. I was amused to notice how obviously awed everyone, including Ellis, was by the prince and princess. Red Wilkens who sat on one side of Oleg and Tom Garrity on the other kept asking the Prince for an explanation of each ribbon and medal. Ellis was next to Katrina and plainly was thrilled. I groaned inwardly when the first course arrived—the ubiquitous baked potato with caviar. I'm sure it was meant as a significant tribute to the Russian guests of honor, but didn't the caterer realize that caviar was hardly a treat to them?

"May I have the butter please, Igor?" I heard Oleg ask.

"Darling," said Katrina, "I think the waiter's name is Arthur. It's hard to read those little name tags without one's glasses," she said with a laugh.

"I want to catch him, too," said Algy. "He forgot to give us chopped onion and egg," he added, obviously trying to display his gourmet tastes.

"Actually, my dear Algernon," said the princess, "I think you will enjoy your caviar more if you add only butter. It is how we Russians eat it. It enables you to better savor the subtle taste."

He looked delighted. I could just hear him instructing his wife to serve caviar at their next dinner party just to give him the opportunity to serve it with only bread and butter. Then he can tell everyone quite casually that this was how Princess Katrina told him it must be done. Visions of becoming the social lion of Saddle River, New Jersey, would surely fill his dreams tonight.

The evening was a smashing success. Mark was besieged by all the young rich lovelies. The presence of their husbands did not preclude hitting on the lord-to-be. In their circles, marriages survive successfully with the acknowledged presence of extramarital activities. When you have everything that money can buy, you have to get your kicks from achieving things that money can't buy, like maybe a small interlude with Michael Jordan, Brad Pitt, or the next Duke of Sandringham. After all, you can't spend your entire day at Bergdorf or Barney's. They would learn quickly that he was staying at the Stanhope. I may have to suggest a change of location.

Cissie came over and gave me a great big hug. "Emma, my sweet, you're one in a million. They won't be able to top this. I raised more money with these seventy people than my competitors take in from their big two-hundred-or-more massive benefits. It will be the affair to top this season."

I looked at her fondly. We go back a while and I have always considered her one of my best and most trustworthy friends. She may come off as flighty and superficial, but down deep she's a rock. She was walking on air—she had pulled off a major coup. She had achieved just what she wanted. And so had I.

XIII

⚜

I DECIDED TO take two days off. I had the time; I hadn't reached my self-imposed two-week deadline yet. I needed the rest. I looked forward to spending time with Mark on my territory. The real truth? I dreaded what I had to do and was indulging myself with a bit of procrastination.

We spent the next day wandering around SoHo and having lunch in this week's hot restaurant, owned by Robert DeNiro. At four o'clock, we were in Rye at my parents' house.

When I had called them on Monday, at the time of my arrival, they were delighted as always to hear that I was finally on their continent.

"When are you coming home for a visit?" asked Dad.

"Yes, dear, we're dying to see you." Mom was on

the other line. Conference calls were now a given.

"I'd like to come Wednesday, but could I bring a friend?"

I heard the hesitation. "Well, dear, of course your friends are always welcome. But we haven't seen you for so long, I thought we could have just a little family get-together to kind of catch up on each other."

I smiled. "Well, O.K., sure. Then I won't bring him."

"Who?" asked my mother, as I knew she would.

"Mark is here with me. I know he would have loved to meet you."

"Mark?" said Mom. "You mean the young earl?"

"The very same."

There was a moment of silence.

"Well of course, bring him, Emma. We would love to have him. Wouldn't we dear?" she asked Dad.

He seemed a bit bewildered by her quick change, but years of practice had taught him to go along with her sudden attitude switches. He knew she would explain later. "Why, sure."

When we arrived, I noticed the parking area in front of the house was packed.

"What's going on?" he asked. "These can't all belong to the staff."

"The staff, as you put it, consists of Conchita Teresa Gonzalez, who came to work for us when she was seventeen, left to get married, and came back last year after her husband died, and now lives here with Mom and Dad. I suspect Mom has asked a few friends to drop by to say hello." I didn't want to tell him he was the stellar attraction.

"What a unique house," he said admiringly. "It's all glass. But in this lovely woodsy setting, I guess you're not too worried about Peeping Toms. Who was the architect?"

"Ulrich Franzen designed it for his family in 1954; it was selected to be the *Architectural Record* House of the Year in 1955 and he went on to fame and fortune as a result. We bought it from him in 1965 and it has spoiled us forever for all conventional houses. Come in and see why."

Mom and Dad were standing at the top of the stone steps on the front deck to greet us. One of the things about a glass house is that no one can sneak up on you. The long driveway coming down toward the house makes every oncoming car totally visible from the glass-walled living room.

"Mom and Dad, this is Mark."

I know my parents well, and I could see they were positively overcome with joy and approval. I enjoyed that; it's nice to give pleasure to people you love. I could see Mark took to them right away, too. But how could you not? They are both outgoing, up-front people whose faces mirror their total contentment and joy in living. My mother has the easy-to-live-with disposition that comes from never allowing minor mishaps to bother her. The kind of niggling details that drive many people into a state of high dudgeon she just shrugs off as the petty issues they are. I have seen friends go into a frothing fit because the postman didn't deliver their mail on time. Or the photo prints they ordered were slightly spotted. Or a bartender put an olive instead of a twist of lemon into the martini.

Dad and I learned from her to put occurrences into their proper perspective, and as a result, we always enjoyed a pleasant easy existence that I have found is rare.

When we came into the forty-five-foot-long glass-walled living room, Mark looked about him with a combination of delight and shock.

"I know," I said quietly. "You love the architecture, but you hate the mob." How my mother managed to get all these people together at a day's notice was incredible. Every friend she had, from bridge, tennis, and work (she teaches English lit. at the State University at Purchase) was there holding drinks and nibbling on hors d'oeuvres being circulated by a smiling Conchita.

"I thought you wouldn't mind if a few of my friends came by just for a drink, Emma dear. They all wanted to see you—you haven't been home for so long."

"Sure, Mom," with a look that told her I wasn't taken in by that line.

"Is your mother trying to make you feel guilty?" Mark whispered in surprise. "She doesn't seem the type."

"No, guilt trips aren't her thing. She's just trying to cover up the fact that she wants the whole world to meet her daughter's boyfriend, the Earl of Chelmsford. We don't get many of those kinds running around Rye."

He was tickled. "My heavens, I'll have to play it broadly. Do we want Lord Peter Wimsey or Bertie Wooster?"

"Why don't we just have Mark Croft? I've always found him quite satisfactory."

He smiled and kissed me lightly on the cheek, an act noticed by everyone in the room, including my beaming parents.

Well trained in the social arts, Mark charmed everyone. If the way he worked the room was an indication of the kind of political candidate he'd be, he's sure to win hands down. There's nothing more effective than a personage who treats people like his equals. Even though they tried to appear nonchalant, I could see that everyone was somewhat awed to meet a titled aristocrat, and delighted and impressed with his friendliness. Every now and then I'd steal looks at my parents and relish their enjoyment. They looked as if they had won the lottery.

After everyone left, we sat down for dinner, just the four of us.

"Well, I think everyone had a good time," said Dad.

"Except for Sally Wilson. She looked like she was sucking on a sour pickle," I said.

"Which one was that?" Mark asked.

"She's the woman who never stops mentioning that her daughter married a Du Pont," said Mom with satisfaction.

Mark and Dad looked puzzled and Mom and I smiled.

As we drove home Mark commented on the easy loving relationship I had with my parents. "I wish my family could behave the same way," he said wistfully. "We all respect and care about each other, but there's no apparent evidence. Displays of emotion are considered bad form, personal issues are rarely discussed.''

"Isn't that due to your public-school education madness that sends little eight-year-old boys away from home never to return except for holidays? The big 'in' word these days is bonding. How could you do it with your parents when you rarely spent time with them?''

"You know, I used to envy the village children who lived home with their families,'' he said. He laughed. "And I was supposed to be the privileged one.''

"My folks really took to you, Mark.''

He looked pleased. "And I to them. I felt totally welcome and at home. Now I can see why you are the wonderful way you are.''

As I dropped him at his hotel I said, "How about breakfast at my place tomorrow? Just give me a buzz when you wake up and I'll have the coffee fresh and hot when you arrive.''

THE NEXT MORNING, after Maria and Francisco cleared the breakfast plates, Oleg, Katrina, Mark, and I took our coffee cups out to the terrace overlooking Central Park. It was a lovely warm spring morning and we all sat enjoying the view. The flowering trees were all in bloom and the place looked like an enchanted forest.

"Katrina, when did you first start working with Red Wilkens?''

There was a stunned silence. Oleg looked at me

with a stricken face. Katrina kept staring at the park. I felt Mark, who was seated next to me, stiffen suddenly.

"I don't think I understand the question," she said calmly.

"I think you do," I said quietly. "You're the autoritet of the Lomonosov *gruoppirovka*. And you enlisted Red Wilkens in your scheme to take over the Tsvetnuye Metalluy."

Oleg had turned white. Katrina merely smiled. "Whatever gave you that idea?" she asked coolly.

"A number of things. My antennae were jangled when I went to Lomonosov with Dmitri Thomasov the first time. When I returned to your house, you asked me to join you for tea because the trip to Lomonosov was undoubtedly so tiring. How did you know where I had been? I had deliberately told no one except Abba."

She kept smiling. "You must have forgotten. You probably told me where you were going."

I shook my head emphatically. "Then there was the iced tea. Where did Raya get the idea that all Americans prefer iced tea? She's partially correct, but it's Americans from the South. In Texas, where Red Wilkens comes from, restaurants continually pour from bottomless pitchers of iced tea throughout the meal."

Katrina laughed. "Raya must have picked that up from the other American southern people we have had as guests."

"But we don't know any other people who speak with that accent," said Oleg in a puzzled voice.

If looks could kill, Oleg would have been an instant

casualty. In a voice filled with disdain, his wife said, "You're an old man and your memory is faulty."

I continued relentlessly, as though there had been no interruptions. "The other evening at the gala, Oleg asked Igor for the butter. You tried to cover up his slip by pretending that he was addressing the waiter whose name tag he had misread. Not so. He was talking to Red, whom he knew as Igor. No one here knows Red's given name, but it's the kind of name he would ask you to call him. It's more dignified and it's Russian."

"She knows, she knows," Oleg said to Katrina, wringing his hands. "I told you we shouldn't have asked her to stay with us."

"Durok!" she said viciously. "Fool—she knows nothing. Keep quiet."

"Is Aleksei involved with you in all this?" I asked.

"Don't you dare try to bring him into this!" she said furiously.

I hit a critical nerve. The mother protecting her cub. "Did you have Irina killed because she was threatening to expose the fact that he raped her when she was twelve?"

"He did not rape her—she enticed him, the little tramp."

Of course, it's never the rapist's fault. The poor guy was being misled and she only got what she deserved.

"He was eighteen, certainly old enough to know having sex with a twelve-year-old child was wrong."

"You didn't see how she dressed," she said with disgust. "Short skirts, tight blouses, she looked like a slut. Then she would hug and kiss him, sit on his lap.''

It was sickening. Her face was contorted not only with anger but envy.

''It was she who seduced him,'' she continued. My Aleksei is an honorable man with a fine reputation. I could not allow her to ruin his good name. Aleksei looks upon her now as a slut,'' she said with satisfaction.

''They had been having sexual relations all these years, up to the day she died.''

''No,'' she said fiercely. ''He told me there has been nothing between them.''

''He lied,'' I said simply.

''My son does not lie to me,'' she said firmly.

''Why not? You lie to him.''

''Never.''

''You said he knows nothing of your Mafia activities. Then you are certainly keeping the truth from him. If you're so honest with him, why didn't you tell him it was you who instructed Berezov to kill her?''

I heard a moan from Oleg.

''It had to be someone who knew they were going to the Kirov that night.''

''This can't be true,'' wailed Oleg. ''Katrina, you had said your association with young Nickonov was only to bring us money. And working with Igor would be a harmless way to help us maintain our house so we wouldn't have to ask Aleksei for money.''

''Your son doesn't have any money to give, Oleg,'' I said. ''He doesn't own the stables at Lomonosov or those horses he talks about. He merely works there.''

"You're wrong. He buys and sells horses," he said querulously.

"Yes—but not his. He is merely an agent for the owners."

"You must be mistaken. What about his big business interests? He is a wealthy man. He gave us the money to buy our house."

I looked at Katrina. "Your wife is the one who provided the money for the house—and for everything else, including the upkeep of your son, enabling him to live the life of a playboy. All those fancy clothes he wears, the expensive restaurants he frequents, all paid for by doting Mama here. With money she gets for running the Lomonosov *gruoppirovka*."

He looked at Katrina in horror. She sat there placidly.

"How did you come to know Nickonov?" I asked.

Oleg answered. "He is the grandson of the man who managed her father's estate. She ran into him one day. I wondered why she has kept up the friendship with such a person."

Finally Katrina couldn't stand it any longer. "You are an idiot, Oleg," she said scornfully. "If it were not for me, we would still be living hand-to-mouth on the charity of others in Estoril. When I saw the millions being made in Russia, I thought why not us? Vladimir presented a God-given opportunity."

Her conceit was staggering. Did she really believe the Almighty would become involved in her nefarious activities?

"He was running a minor Mafia group—all they dealt in were small cafés and bars. To him and his family, I will always be the princess and he would do as I told him. It was easy to enlist him."

"How did you meet Red Wilkens?" I asked.

"Aleksei brought him home for tea. He had come to Aleksei's stables and liked him at once. Everyone likes Aleksei," she said proudly. "When I asked him what he was doing in St. Petersburg, he told me about the factory they were going to pour millions of dollars into. I told him that some Mafia *gruoppirovka* would surely show up to take their share. And then I thought, why not us? I brought up the subject with him, and he was enthusiastic. He came to visit us a few times and we worked out the details."

"Why did you bring Nickonov into it?"

"We needed a *gruoppirovka* to handle the enforcement details and to protect us from other Mafia. I took over the organization, of course. Vladimir has big muscles but small brains. He was delighted with the arrangement. Why not? I have brought him into what you Americans call the 'big time.' "

"Why are you telling her all this, Katrina? She will go to the police," said Oleg hysterically.

"And then what?" asked his wife with a smug smile. "They cannot touch us. We are Russian citizens and we have committed no crime on American soil."

"Then you won't mind answering more questions," I said.

"Not at all," said Katrina, sitting back contentedly. "In fact, I am enjoying this. The whole operation has been vastly successful and I've had no one to tell about it."

"You said no competitive Mafia would interfere with your deal with the Tsvetnuye Metalluy. Then why did you have Stanislaus Chirkasov killed?"

Oleg groaned.

"I learned that his *gruoppirovka*, the Tambovskaya Mafia, was planning to take over our factory. Based solely on Mr. Chirkasov's expertise and talents, they were building an industrial empire that would shortly bury us. The quickest way to stop them was to eliminate him."

"Just like that—as though he was a sick horse who must be put down. He had a mother, father, and sister who loved him."

She shrugged. "My dear Emma. This is not a tea party—it's a war, serious business. There must naturally be casualties."

"Now you are planning to become the industrial empire builder. Professor Yakolov will be your engineering expert, right?"

Mark sat up. He had been listening quietly, his expression a mixture of shock and distaste. This was the part I was going to hate.

"You figured that out, did you? I always told Oleg that you were very sharp. I was hoping you and Aleksei—well, you would be just the strength he needs. I'm afraid he inherited his father's weakness, more's the pity," she said, looking disdainfully at the now totally crushed Oleg.

"Did you know about the professor's economic theory of government?" I continued.

She laughed. "That childish nonsense? Of course, I let him rant and rave. It was harmless and it allowed him to develop the devoted following of young starry-eyed idiots who he obviously enjoyed and we were able to use."

I sighed inwardly. Here goes. "How about his new fantastic software invention?" Mark's face turned red and he leaned forward.

"The instant E-mail translator? More foolish dreaming. When Irina told me her beloved professor was working on something marvelous, I went to see him. He showed it to me and said it would take years to produce. We are not into long-term development, but I saw that it could produce large sums right now if sold to the right starry-eyed idiot investor."

I didn't look at Mark.

"When I explained the potential and told him my plan, he protested, stating the importance of his scholarly honor. When he heard how much money he would get, his great scientist's ethics disappeared," she said scathingly. "He even found the right investor, whose identity he has refused to divulge. It is one of Anatoly's small-minded traits—he loves to have secrets."

I saw Mark sink back into his chair. "Did Anatoly's students know about the professor's project?"

"Yes, all his foolish little followers knew. But they thought he devised the whole scheme to promote his ridiculous economic program."

I was surprised. "You mean they know the enterprise is fraudulent?"

She laughed. "You seem shocked, my poor Emma.

You are as blindly naive as they are. They are so besotted with their so-called cause that they are perfectly willing to close their eyes to the source of any subsidizing that comes their way. The means don't matter—it is only the ends they care about. To them this project only increases their devotion to Anatoly; they see only the cleverness and not the chicanery. That is the way of zealots. As for me, I freely admit that I do what I do to make money for me. Am I not therefore more honest than they?''

I couldn't believe I was getting a lecture on morality from a cold-blooded murderer. And worse, it had validity.

"So Anatoly never intends to produce his revolutionary software?"

She laughed. "Of course not. He doesn't have a clue about the technology needed to create this product."

"You mean when he gets the investor's money, he intends just to take it and run?"

"Yes—to us. We will give him his share."

"And he's willing to accept that when it's his idea?"

"My dear Emma. Ideas are a dime a dozen. It's the execution that counts. Where do you think he got the expertise to prepare the proposal, spreadsheet, and projections? Where do you think he got the financing to create those instant translations to impress and fool the potential investor?"

Mark's face made me feel sick. But I had to go on. "Irina was a very idealistic young woman. Somehow I cannot see her going along with such an unconscionable scheme, even though she believed it would produce profits that would go into bettering the state of her country,'' I said.

Katrina's face became a mask of hate. ''She didn't know at first. When she found out it was all a fake, she carried on about the whole thing being wrong. Imagine that trollop talking about immorality?''

''And that's another reason you had her killed.''

''Of course. I had no choice. Anatoly came to me in a very agitated state. Irina had questioned him about the production details of his miraculous invention and apparently had enough computer knowledge to see the flaws in it. When she realized the whole thing was a a fraud intended only to make Anatoly rich, she got furious and announced she would inform the prospective investor. I could not allow that. She was nothing but a worthless whore anyway.''

Her total amorality was horrifying. ''Of course you would know about whores,'' I said. ''You employ so many of them in Helsinki.''

''What is she saying, Katrina?'' asked Oleg.

''She is talking about one of the businesses that allow you to live so well, my dear,'' she said to her husband.

''Does Aleksei know you were responsible for his cousin's death?''

''No, why should he be troubled with such information? Like his father, he has never asked about the source of our money.''

''How much was it that you and Red Wilkens siphoned off so far from the Brannock Foundation's investment in the Tsvetnuye Metalluy?''

She smiled broadly. "According to our accountant's latest report, I believe it was ten million dollars."

I heard someone gasp. It was me.

"I assume you would like us to leave your home, Emma," said Katrina.

"Yes."

Katrina arose. "Come, Oleg. Let's pack."

"Are you returning to Russia?" I asked.

"Not yet. We have many invitations to stay with people we met last night. It was really quite a lovely affair and I thank you for arranging it," she said with a gloating smile. "We'll return home next week as planned." As she was leaving the room she turned to me. "I gather the Brannock Foundation was the sponsor. It is ironic, isn't it, that what I assume will be the end of our relationship should find them once again my benefactor?"

What a positively hateful woman. If she hadn't been eighty years old, I think I might have decked her. I know that physical force isn't supposed to achieve anything, but it sure as hell would have made me feel better.

"You realize I intend to turn all this information over to RUOP and the general prosecutor's office in Moscow," I said.

She looked at me coolly. "Go right ahead. We will just increase our monthly payments to them and the whole matter will be conveniently overlooked."

After they left the room, Mark looked at me. "You knew."

I nodded. "I couldn't tell you. People no longer

kill the bearers of bad tidings, but they sure would like to. I wanted you to hear the truth about the professor's swindle from someone else. And I wanted you to be out of Russia when you did. You were dealing with a group of people who do not take rejection well.''

"So I heard," he said with a little shiver. "Now what are you going to do about that horrible woman and Mr. Wilkens?"

"Let me work on it for a while," I said.

I MET WITH Ellis Brannock in his office the following day and gave him my report. I started with Katrina's activities.

"The foul bitch!" he said. "I can't believe that perfect lady is a ruthless killer." Then he got really agitated. "And she'll get away with everything. In that lawless country, they'll never even arrest her, let alone put her on trial. And what really burns my ass is that it's my money she's using to pay off everyone in their corrupt law-enforcement system to keep her from being prosecuted.''

He stewed for a few minutes and then asked, "She was working with someone on my board. O.K.—who was it?"

"Red Wilkens."

He sat so stone still that I thought he died. "Are you absolutely sure?" he asked in a flat voice.

"Both Katrina and Oleg spoke of his frequent visits.''

"Can we believe those immoral thieving sons of bitches?"

What's going on here? I thought. Why is he finding it so difficult to accept?

"I checked the airlines and found that Red Wilkens has flown to St. Petersburg five times in the past six months."

"You couldn't get that information. The airlines don't give it out."

"Look, Ellis, your distrust is becoming annoying. I don't usually divulge my methods or sources, because it isn't any of your damned business how I achieve results, as long as I do. However, since for some reason you seem loath to accept my word, a detective chief superintendent of the Finnish National Bureau of Investigation accessed Finnair's passenger lists for me. If you want the dates of Red's flights from New York to Helsinki and Helsinki to St. Petersburg, I'll be happy to supply them. And his seat numbers, too."

He fell back in his chair and looked at me apologetically. "I'm sorry. I didn't mean to doubt you. It's just I couldn't believe it." Suddenly his face turned purple and he jumped up from his chair and got so furious I thought he would have a stroke.

"That miserable son of a bitch. We've been friends for twenty-five years. I was best man at his wedding— one of them, that is. I am the godfather of one of his kids. When he had a not-too-small cash-flow problem some years ago, I bailed him out. That's how the motherfucker thanks me—by taking me for ten million dollars? I swear I'll kill the bastard."

"Fine, but legally," I said. "When I see you again, I don't want it to be through wire mesh at the penitentiary. There are better ways to punish someone other than death.''

He calmed down and sat back at his desk. ''How?''

''Just turn the feds on him. You don't think he paid income tax on the money he stole, do you? They'll easily nail him for that. Plus embezzlement for misdirecting Foundation money into his own pocket. Death is a quickie. But long years in prison provide a protracted misery that's far worse punishment. And for sure he'll be forced to make some restitution to you, which may mean that much of the money will be restored to the foundation. I doubt if he spent all his ill-gotten millions in this short a time.''

''You know,'' he said, ''when you told me one of my board was misappropriating Foundation funds, I checked into the financial positions of every one of them. I found Martina's company was in some trouble. So I figured it was her.''

O.K., reader—who did you think it was?

''I never thought of Red. His business is in tip-top shape, which means his stock is worth a large fortune and his income is astronomical. Like me, he's got more money than he could ever use in five lifetimes and enough to leave all his children millionaires. He and I used to talk about guys like Boesky and Milken and wonder why they did what they did and how much is enough. It makes no sense,'' he said, shaking his head. ''What would make him get involved with this shitty, dangerous business and betray a friend to boot? I could see if he was lured into it by some seductive young piece of ass. He's the vulnerable age. The princess may have been a stunner sixty years ago, but now she's hardly what one would regard as a sex object. So why?''

"Maybe it just seemed so easy. Red is an oil man—they're big gamblers and enjoy risk taking. Now he's retired, bored, feeling old and obsolete. This may have seemed like a challenge and high adventure, working with the deadly Russian Mafia. Perhaps it was the kind of youthful excitement he craved, a way to prove to himself that he's still got it.''

Ellis looked so forlorn and sad that I felt like hugging him to my bosom and saying "there, there." But I thought it might be more prudent to opt for humor to avoid complications. "Or maybe he saw himself as a reverse Robin Hood. Stealing from the poor and giving it to the rich.''

He smiled and then opened his desk drawer and pulled out a checkbook. This is the part I always enjoy.

He wrote quickly and handed me a check, which I tucked into my handbag without inspecting it. I consider it bad form to read a check when it's handed to you, because this implies you don't trust the giver to have delivered the correct amount.

"Aren't you going to look at it?" Ellis asked.

"It's poor manners to doubt one's clients.''

"Suppose I gave you less than you expected?''

"I'm polite, Ellis, but I'm not an idiot. I'll look at the check the minute I'm outside your door. If it's wrong, I'll be back in a shot.''

"Look now," he said.

I took it out of my bag and glanced at it. Fifty thousand dollars!

"I figured that would make you happy," he said as he observed my beaming face. "I don't give away money for nothing, as you have undoubtedly heard. But you did a helluva job and I believe in fair compensation to people who work for me."

"Thank you. I appreciate the vote of confidence and I love the money."

"I also paid you more to soften you up, Emma. I'm generous but rarely without a reason. I want you to take Red's place as a permanent member of the board."

I was taken aback. "I don't know, Ellis. I approve of your goals, but I'm a working woman. I don't have time for meetings and whatever duties are required. The others are all retired. For me it could cause a sizable drop in income."

"Of course, I understand," he said.

I could see him thinking.

"I'll tell you what. I'll create for you the corporate position of charity consultant for Brannock Industries to oversee my giving activities. Your job will be to supervise the Brannock Foundation, for which you will be paid an annual salary of one hundred and twenty thousand dollars, ten thousand a month. All it will entail is attending meetings and controlling the direction of the Foundation's distributions and making sure everything is kosher. That should compensate you for any income you might lose."

I was stunned. Then I thought for a moment. "Would that mean I could arrange for specific allocations that are proper for the mission of the Foundation?"

"Exactly."

"O.K. Then I would like the Brannock Foundation to make a major donation of however many millions are required to improve Russia's justice system. This would take the form of subsidizing huge increases in salaries to every member of law-enforcement and justice departments in specific major cities, such as Moscow and St. Petersburg, for the next five years. That would include police, judges, prosecuting officers, and fees for lawyers. This would be contingent upon their prosecuting every miscreant, male or female, rich or poor, who has committed a serious crime. Any indication that any case has been deliberately overlooked or mishandled due to private payoffs will negate the entire program immediately. Which means every member of the law-enforcement system in Russia had better watch every other member because one person's misstep would remove the gravy train for everyone."

Ellis looked at me for a few seconds and then broke into a roar of laughter. "You're a genius! Not only will that guarantee our killer princess will be brought to justice—but I will look like the most brilliant benefactor since Turner donated millions to the UN and Soros gave money to retrain the military." He bounced around the room with elation. "It's for sure going to get me on page one of the *New York Times*, maybe even the Man of the Year cover of *Time*. Emma, how would you like to be my lawyer, too? You've got the kind of inventive divergent-thinking mind I need."

I smiled with satisfaction. "Thanks but no thanks. Been there, done that, had it."

"Pity," said Ellis, "but I'll take you on any terms. We have a deal, then. You're a permanent member of the board, and you can implement your new program immediately."

I CELEBRATED WITH Mark that evening. I would have gladly picked up the check in the fanciest restaurant in the city, but the best food in New York comes out of Maria's kitchen in my home. We enjoyed a splendid meal in the plush privacy of my dining room and then sat on the terrace after dinner sipping Veuve-Clicquot champagne. He had listened avidly to my recounting of my visit with Ellis. When I came to the plan for subsidizing the Russian justice system, he shouted "Hear, Hear" with absolute glee.

"That's brilliant, absolutely super. Now how will you get things going to indict Katrina?"

"Simple. As soon as Ellis's lawyers and accountants get through drawing up the proposal, and the PR department makes the announcement, I'll phone Sledovatel Ivan Golov, the detective in the St. Petersburg Police Department who is handling the case of Irina's murder. I will also talk to the general prosecutor's office, the Federal Security Bureau, and of course, RUOP. Then I'll just sit back and watch with pleasure."

He looked at me admiringly. "You're devious but adorable." A shadow crossed his face. "Now I understand thoroughly what you do, darling, and why it is so fulfilling," he said. "Actually, you do so much good in the world that it would be a shame to give it up."

He paused for a few seconds. "I envy you and I'm proud of you."

"And you understand why marrying you is so difficult for me to consider," I said softly.

He reached over and took my hand. "Oh, I won't give up on that. When two people feel the way we do about each other, there has to be some arrangement we can work out to keep us together. Will you be going over to Russia to become involved in the princess's prosecution?"

"No way. I'd be out of my mind to do that. When the Mafia gets wind of my reform program for Russia's law and order, which may lead to putting all of them out of business, I'll be on every hit list in town. Communication can be quite effective today with fax, phone, and E-mail."

"Will they have enough evidence to convict Katrina?"

"I believe so. I'll ask the Finns to offer a plea-bargain deal with Berezov to possibly reduce his sentence if he testifies in a Russian court that Katrina gave him the orders to kill both Irina and Stosh. I don't think they'll ever get Nickonov to say a word against his princess. His awe and respect for her and her family are too ingrained. But I think Red Wilkens will be glad to get on a Russian stand to atone for his sins. What the hell; it can't make his position any worse and it could maybe make it better. That kind of act sits well with an American judge when it comes to Red's sentencing.''

I saw him looking at me. ''You look tired, my love. It's been quite a day for you. I think you should get to bed now.''

I looked at him mischievously. ''You mean before I become too tired?''

''That, too.''

Mark had taken over the guest room that the prince and princess had vacated. Now that the room was available, it seemed ridiculous for him to pay those exorbitant New York hotel prices. Also he needed to be out of reach of all the young social set who must be clogging the phone lines at the Stanhope right now.

As we lay in bed in postcoital relaxation he said, ''Lord, I'm going to miss you.''

''You're leaving soon?'' I asked.

''Yes, I have some matters coming up in London on Friday and I must be there, worse luck.''

I was disappointed. After a case, especially one as intense as this one, I like to take some weeks off and I had been hoping to enjoy them here with Mark.

He ran his hand caressingly over my back. ''Couldn't you see your way clear to possibly popping over to London for a bit?''

Why not? After all, my wonderful King's Road flat is there just waiting for me. And my English pals have been nagging me to come over. And I would be right on time for the spectacular Chelsea Flower Show, which is walking distance from my flat and draws people from all over the world.

"I'll think about it," I answered. That's what my mother always said when I used to plead for something. Except that her "I'll think about it" meant "no" and was just to get me off her back. With Mark, I meant quite the opposite.